A Candlelight Ecstasy Romance

"DON'T EVER LET HIM STOP!" SHE CRIED SILENTLY.

Slowly Hunter released her. She looked up at him in confusion, then blushed in mortification as she realized what had just happened. She had wanted Hunter to go on kissing her, holding her, touching her! Aghast, she pulled away from him and walked across the floor on unsteady legs.

"Marilyn, look at me," Hunter said softly.

Slowly she turned and looked at him with wide round eyes. Hunter was breathing as hard as she was, his eyes covered with the fine glaze of passion.

"You can come back to life," he said simply. "For a few moments there in my arms you did."

Without giving her a chance to reply, he turned on his heel and left the house, slamming the door behind him.

"Damn you, Hunter Templeton," Marilyn whispered at his retreating back. "Why won't you leave me alone?"

A CANDLELIGHT ECSTASY ROMANCE®

178 A SUMMER'S EMBRACE, *Cathie Linz*
179 DESERT SPLENDOR, *Samantha Hughes*
180 LOST WITHOUT LOVE, *Elizabeth Raffel*
181 A TEMPTING STRANGER, *Lori Copeland*
182 DELICATE BALANCE, *Emily Elliott*
183 A NIGHT TO REMEMBER, *Shirley Hart*
184 DARK SURRENDER, *Diana Blayne*
185 TURN BACK THE DAWN, *Nell Kincaid*
186 GEMSTONE, *Bonnie Drake*
187 A TIME TO LOVE, *Jackie Black*
188 WINDSONG, *Jo Calloway*
189 LOVE'S MADNESS, *Sheila Paulos*
190 DESTINY'S TOUCH, *Dorothy Ann Bernard*
191 NO OTHER LOVE, *Alyssa Morgan*
192 THE DEDICATED MAN, *Lass Small*
193 MEMORY AND DESIRE, *Eileen Bryan*
194 A LASTING IMAGE, *Julia Howard*
195 RELUCTANT MERGER, *Alexis Hill Jordan*
196 GUARDIAN ANGEL, *Linda Randall Wisdom*
197 DESIGN FOR DESIRE, *Anna Hudson*
198 DOUBLE PLAY, *Natalie Stone*
199 SENSUOUS PERSUASION, *Eleanor Woods*
200 MIDNIGHT MEMORIES, *Emily Elliott*
201 DARING PROPOSAL, *Tate McKenna*
202 REACH FOR THE STARS, *Sara Jennings*
203 A CHARMING STRATEGY, *Cathie Linz*
204 AFTER THE LOVING, *Samantha Scott*
205 DANCE FOR TWO, *Kit Daley*
206 THE MAN WHO CAME TO STAY, *Margot Prince*
207 BRISTOL'S LAW, *Rose Marie Ferris*
208 PLAY TO WIN, *Shirley Hart*
209 DESIRABLE COMPROMISE, *Suzanne Sherrill*
210 LOVERS' KNOT, *Hayton Monteith*
211 TENDER JOURNEY, *Margaret Dobson*
212 ALL OUR TOMORROWS, *Lori Herter*
213 LOVER IN DISGUISE, *Gwen Fairfax*
214 TENDER DECEPTION, *Heather Graham*
215 MIDNIGHT MAGIC, *Barbara Andrews*
216 WINDS OF HEAVEN, *Karen Whittenburg*
217 ALL OR NOTHING, *Lori Copeland*

MORNING'S PROMISE

Emily Elliott

Published by
Dell Publishing Co., Inc.
1 Dag Hammarskjold Plaza
New York, New York 10017

Copyright © 1984 by Emily Mims

All rights reserved. No part of this book may be
reproduced or transmitted in any form or by any
means, electronic or mechanical, including photocopying,
recording or by any information storage
and retrieval system, without the written permission
of the Publisher, except where permitted by law.

Dell ® TM 681510, Dell Publishing Co., Inc.

Candlelight Ecstasy Romance®, 1,203,540, is a registered
trademark of Dell Publishing Co., Inc., New York, New
York.

ISBN: 0-440-15829-X

Printed in the United States of America
First printing—March 1984

To Our Readers:

We have been delighted with your enthusiastic response to Candlelight Ecstasy Romances®, and we thank you for the interest you have shown in this exciting series.

In the upcoming months we will continue to present the distinctive sensuous love stories you have come to expect only from Ecstasy. We look forward to bringing you many more books from your favorite authors and also the very finest work from new authors of contemporary romantic fiction.

As always, we are striving to present the unique, absorbing love stories that you enjoy most—books that are more than ordinary romance.

Your suggestions and comments are always welcome. Please write to us at the address below.

Sincerely,

The Editors
Candlelight Romances
1 Dag Hammarskjold Plaza
New York, New York 10017

CHAPTER ONE

Why does all wedding cake taste the same? Hunter Templeton wondered as he politely swallowed the last bite of the fluffy white concoction. *I got better dessert than this when I was in the navy.* Trying hard not to let the boredom that he felt show in his expression, he leaned against the wall and surveyed the reception hall casually, practicing putting names with faces so that when he met the various members of his new congregation on the street he wouldn't embarrass himself and hurt anyone's feelings by not remembering just exactly who he was talking to. In a few months he would know every name, face, and family connection with no problem, but for the first month or two in a new church, it was hard.

The bride and groom, of course, were Janette and Tom Grainger, the son and daughter of two of New Braunfels's most illustrious families. They were combining two medium-sized ranches into one rather large one with their union, and both sets of parents were well-pleased. Hunter's eyes left the bride and groom and traveled the room, putting a name with most of the faces. Tonya Schriever, the pretty, giggling maid of honor. Joe and Irene Tate, the mother and father of the bride. Myra Grainger, the groom's widowed mother. Hank Schriever, his garrulous old elder, who made it his business to know the business of everybody in New Braunfels. Hunter's brow wrinkled as he looked searchingly at the face of the young woman who was standing with Hank. He could not put a name with her face.

Hunter frowned. He had been in his new post for over a month now, and he was certain that today was the first time he had ever seen this particular young woman. She was tall, slender without being too thin, had good legs, and wore her raven hair clouding around her face and falling almost to her shoulders. Yes, if he had seen her before, he definitely would have remembered her. The last moments before the ceremony were always a blur, but he thought she had been playing the organ for the wedding. If it had been her, she was certainly a fine musician. She was not a professional, but she had a definite flair, and she had sounded much better than the regular organist. Mrs. Weissmann was sincere and tried hard, but her arthritic fingers simply were no longer up to playing for an entire service.

As subtly as he could, he surveyed the young woman through lowered lids. Hank Schriever had left her alone and now an older woman was talking to her. As the young woman smiled and nodded at something that the older woman said, Hunter felt the breath catch in his throat as something in him responded to the woman's smile. *Is she married?* Hunter wondered with more than idle interest. *Who is she? And why isn't she playing for the church on a regular basis?*

His curiosity getting the better of him, Hunter wandered idly in the direction of the dark-haired woman, trying not to make his interest in her too obvious. He would start with her name and take a peek at her left hand, although if she were married, she would probably volunteer that information right away—most happily married women did. He lingered just within earshot of the women and wondered idly if his interest in her was purely in the hope of getting a better organist for the church. Then he glanced down her slender body, letting his gaze linger on her legs, and assured himself that his music program was the least of his concern at the moment. *But maybe,* he mused, *if I can get her to come and play for us, I'll see her again.*

Finally the older woman drifted away, leaving her standing by herself, an expression of bitter sadness passing fleetingly across her face, to be replaced quickly with polite interest as she saw Hunter approaching. Wondering about the expression that he was sure he had seen, Hunter extended his hand and shook hers warmly. "I'm Hunter Templeton," he said softly. "I don't believe we've met."

"Marilyn Davis," she said in a husky contralto voice. "Your service was delightful tonight," she added as she removed her hand from his. He noted gratefully that she wore no wedding ring.

Hunter felt the pulse in his neck start to throb as her delicious perfume tantalized his nostrils. "Why don't we get a cup of punch?" he asked as he took her arm, covered with a gauzy fabric, and led her toward the punch bowl.

A smiling teenager with a carnation corsage handed them both a cup of punch. "Here you are, Reverend Templeton." She smiled as she dripped a little of the sticky pink liquid on his hand.

Hunter smiled and vowed not to eat anything else sweet for a week. The girl smiled at Marilyn and handed her a cup of punch. "It's good to see you, Mrs. Davis," the girl said. "It's been a long time."

Mrs.? Hunter thought with disappointed surprise. He checked her hand again and mentally shrugged. Probably she was divorced. At least he hoped so.

Marilyn smiled at the girl, but Hunter could have sworn he saw a hint of sadness in her eye. "Yes, it has, hasn't it?" she replied lightly. "Janey, aren't you about ready to graduate?"

"Sure am, Mrs. Davis," the girl said proudly.

"Good for you!" Marilyn smiled. "Keep up the good work, Janey."

Janey nodded. "I'm thinking about going to work for the sheriff's department," the girl said confidingly. "What do you think?"

"We'd love to have you on the force," Marilyn said encouragingly. "Come on down a little closer to graduation and I'll show you the ropes." Marilyn smiled again at the girl and collected a piece of cake.

"Did I hear you correctly?" Hunter asked Marilyn when they were seated in the folding chairs that lined the walls. "You're a deputy sheriff?"

"Sure am," Marilyn said as she took a bite of the cake. She grimaced and put her fork down. "I just can't eat this," she said as she set the plate on the empty chair next to her. She watched the crowd with a pleasant expression on her face, but Hunter could have sworn that there was sadness lurking beneath the surface, although it certainly did not show on the outside. "So, are you learning to like our little town?" she asked mildly.

"It sure beats Houston," Hunter replied frankly.

Marilyn laughed out loud. "I certainly hope so," she said. "Seriously, are you settling in all right? Everything at the church okay?"

"Nearly everything," Hunter replied frankly. "Sunday school's growing, visitation's going great guns, and the elders are a great bunch to work with," he added. "There's only one problem, and that's in the music department." He felt rather than saw Marilyn stiffen beside him.

"Oh?" she asked, a little too casually.

"Yes," Hunter replied warily, wondering what had made her react to the comment about the music like that. "Mrs. Weissmann is having a great deal of trouble playing the service. I was wondering . . ."

"Excuse me, Reverend Templeton," Marilyn said abruptly, her face freezing before she could school it to politeness. She quickly composed herself and stood up rapidly and would have fled across the room but for the hand that Hunter laid on her arm.

"Just a minute," Hunter said quickly before she could get away. "I would like to talk to you before you go." He looked up and was surprised to find the look of a cornered rabbit on her face, but rather than let her get away, he pulled her back down gently into the seat beside him. Hunter could tell that Marilyn was rearranging her face into wary politeness. "I just wanted to see if you would consider playing for us on Sunday. I know that this is short notice . . ."

"I'm afraid not," Marilyn replied too quickly. "I'm working this Sunday."

"Well, perhaps the Sunday after that?" Hunter pressed on, ignoring the shuttered look that crossed her face. His interest in her was not strictly in getting a good organist. If she were to play for the church, he could be sure of seeing her again.

"No," Marilyn replied curtly, then caught herself and colored a little. "I have to work on Sundays," she continued politely. "I'm sorry, I can't." Hunter could not be sure, but he could have sworn that there was something besides her job behind her point-blank refusal to play for him.

"Very well then," he said abruptly, disappointed that he would have no excuse to see her again. "It was nice to meet you, Mrs. Davis," he said, his glance going down to her bare left hand. "Or is it Miss?" he corrected himself.

"Take your choice," Marilyn replied quietly. "I'm divorced." She picked up her cup and sipped the sweet punch. "It was nice to meet you," she added as an elderly couple rushed up and embraced her warmly.

Hunter nodded and walked away from her, a frown of puzzlement marring his features. She seemed nice enough, but there was an aura of sadness, of bitterness, around her that she could not hide entirely, although he sensed that she was trying to do so. And her point-blank refusal to play for services puzzled him, since she was obviously an experienced organist, and most musicians loved to play every chance they got. *I don't understand it,* he thought. *But I'll bet that I can find somebody who's willing to indulge in a little gossip, if I try hard enough!* he thought wickedly.

How much longer can this reception drag on? Marilyn wondered as she gagged down a bite of wedding cake and plastered a smile on her face for dear old Mrs. Borrer. The little old lady chattered on, oblivious to the fact that Marilyn's nerves were at the screaming point. Marilyn briefly considered making her excuses and leaving early, but she felt that might hurt Myra Grainger's feelings, and she did not want to do that. Besides, since her parents had retired to their vacation home on the coast, Marilyn was her family's representative at the wedding and therefore would have to stay. *But I'm not coming within a mile of this place for the next year,* she promised herself as she smiled a little grimly. Playing for the wedding had been bad enough, but the new minister's asking her to play for the church again had been almost too much to take. Jerking her mind back to Mrs. Borrer, Marilyn willed herself to listen politely and make small talk, determinedly holding up her polite social facade, hoping that her old friends could not see just how upset she was tonight.

Surreptitiously she glanced over at the new bachelor preacher who had set every loose tongue in New Braunfels wagging. And no wonder! If ever a man did not fit the stereotype minister, this one didn't. Tall, broad-shouldered, slim-hipped, this man looked as though he would be more at home on one of the local ranches or maybe at a construction site than in a church. Too rough-hewn to be called handsome, his carelessly chiseled face nevertheless compelled her to look at him yet again. Wide cheekbones gave his face an almost Slavic look, and his firm, well-shaped mouth spoke of intense determination and latent sensuality. But it was his eyes that had almost thrown Marilyn into a panic. Dark, almost black, hooded by thick brows, they contrasted sharply with the man's light blond, graying hair that faded into red at the sideburns. Those eyes seemed able to bore into her very soul. The revival preachers of old must have had eyes like that, she thought. Eyes that seared all that they surveyed. As his were surveying her right now, a look of frowning puzzlement on his face.

I'll bet he's not used to having people telling him no, Marilyn thought with grim amusement as the photographer called for the bride and groom to come to the middle of the room to throw the bouquet and the garter. All he probably has to do was stare with that penetrating gaze into his congregation's eyes, and they're at his beck and call. Or he might just have to smile at the women, she thought as she caught him smiling winningly at one of the elders' wives. Admitting to herself that under other circumstances she might have been equally swayed by his charm, Marilyn turned her attention to the activity in the middle of the room. All the young and not-so-young single women clustered behind the bride. Awkwardly the young girl tossed the large bouquet over her shoulder and right into the arms of her fifteen-year-old sister.

The guests clapped and laughed when Irene Tate called to her younger daughter to "give it back!" Marilyn felt Hunter looking across the room at her, but she did not trust herself to return his gaze. Instead, she turned and willed herself to speak to one of her old friends from high school, who promptly asked if Marilyn would join her and her husband for dinner sometime. Marilyn nodded politely and started to suggest a date, but remembered the couple's infant daughter and stopped herself.

Next, the thin young groom knelt and amid applause and whistles slipped the garter down his new wife's shapely leg. *Robert got mine caught on the heel of my shoe,* Marilyn remembered suddenly, sadness piercing through her. She forced herself to laugh and clapped determinedly as the handsome best man, something of a young rake, caught the garter.

Thankfully, the bride and groom went away to change, and Marilyn breathed a sigh of relief. They would be leaving soon, and she could drop this facade of politeness, and escape to her little home to be alone with her thoughts. Rising and putting her cake plate on the table, she accepted a rice bag from the little flower girl and waited anxiously for the bride and groom to reappear. Premonition prickling her neck, she turned around to see Myra Grainger bearing down on her, with Hunter at her heels.

"Oh, Marilyn, I just had to come over and tell you how much I enjoyed your music!" Myra Grainger piped as Marilyn whirled around hastily. The tiny birdlike woman threw her thin arms around Marilyn and hugged her soundly. "It was just like in the old days before, well, when you used to play for us all the time." Myra turned to Hunter. "Reverend Templeton, doesn't Marilyn play beautifully? Why, Irene Tate and I were just talking about how much we missed hearing you play." Hunter turned accusing eyes on Marilyn and she flinched. "And we said that New Braunfels hadn't seen such a pretty wedding since yours and Robert's."

Marilyn gasped at Myra's heedless comment and smiled grimly. "You just better hope this one lasts a little longer than mine did, Myra," she said, dropping her social mask for a moment and giving both Myra and Hunter a glimpse of her inner misery. "Myra, would you forgive me if I left now? I have to be up early tomorrow." Actually she did not have to be on duty until the middle of the afternoon, but she had taken just about as much of this gathering as she could stand.

"Of course," Myra said quietly as she hugged Marilyn gently. "See you soon, love," she said as Marilyn broke away and strode purposefully toward the door. Myra turned to Hunter and shrugged helplessly. "Depend on me to put my foot in it," she said as her mouth tightened. "I guess I upset her but good."

"Do you think I should follow her and make sure she's all right?" Hunter asked.

Myra nodded. "Thanks, Reverend Templeton."

Fighting back tears, Marilyn made her way through the crisp fall air to her pickup truck and slumped into the seat, staring with unseeing eyes straight in front of her. On the whole, she hadn't done too badly. She had gotten through the wedding all right, and had almost made it through the reception, too, until Myra made those thoughtless comments about her happier days. Tears welled in her eyes and she groped around in her purse for a tissue, then remembered that she did not have any. She sniffed back the tears, then felt around in her purse for the truck keys.

"Can you use this?" a deep voice asked as Hunter dangled a handkerchief in front of her window.

Marilyn looked up, startled, into Hunter Templeton's compassionate face. "Thanks, I could," she said as she dabbed at her eyes and blew her nose. She handed the handkerchief back to Hunter and then turned back to her purse and felt around for the keys, then stared in surprise as Hunter took the purse from her hand and swiftly located her key ring. She took it from him and put the key in the ignition, then realized that she could not start the truck, since Hunter was leaning against the fender. The cab was fairly high off the ground and Hunter's eyes were only a few inches above her own. They bore into her with the heat of two coals, probing her with such intensity that it was all Marilyn could do to stay in the driver's seat and not slide across to the other door and run into the darkness.

"Tonight's been hard on you, hasn't it?" Hunter asked quietly.

Marilyn nodded. "And I thought I had hidden it so well," she replied dryly.

"Oh, I think you did," Hunter said sincerely. "Tell me, was it memories of your own wedding that were upsetting you so?"

Marilyn shook her head. "Not—not really," she stammered, although she had thought of her own wedding a couple of times this evening. "Reverend Templeton, would you forgive me if I said that I don't want to go into it with you tonight?" she almost pleaded into his piercing dark eyes. "I've really had enough."

"Of course," Hunter replied, stepping back from the truck. "Another time, perhaps?"

Marilyn nodded, knowing that she had no intention of ever talking to Hunter Templeton about it. "Good night," she said simply as she switched on the ignition and backed out of the parking place.

There goes one brave lady, Hunter thought as he watched Marilyn drive away into the cool autumn night. She must have just put in a miserable evening, but from her behavior at the reception, you would have thought she didn't have a care in the world. Hunter acknowledged to himself that the attraction that he had felt for her earlier this evening was now joined by a feeling of intense curiosity. Determined not to leave the reception until he had some answers, Hunter walked back into the reception hall and picked up another cup of punch, smiling at Janey as he took it from her. "Have you seen Hank Schriever around here?" he asked casually.

The girl looked embarrassed. "I think he went out on the walkway," she said as she turned to fill another cup.

Hunter stifled a smile. Hank and half of his elders smoked like chimneys, but they would rather eat their cigarettes than smoke in the church building. Thanking the girl, he slipped out the other door of the reception hall into the cool autumn air. He peered into the gloom and saw Hank's solitary figure staring over into the cemetery, smoking a glowing cigarette. "Hank?" he called out quietly.

"That you, Hunter?" Hank asked, moving swiftly to put out his cigarette.

Hunter smiled at the use of his first name. Although he had invited the elders to use his first name, Hank was the first one to do so. Hunter reached out and stilled the arm that was about to throw down the cigarette. "Go ahead and enjoy your smoke," he said softly. The two men stood together in the still autumn air. "Hank, how well do you know Marilyn Davis?" he asked suddenly. Hunter did not believe in wasting time on small talk.

"She's my goddaughter," Hank said softly. "Otis and Maggie White's girl. Not such a girl these days though. Must be pushing thirty."

Hunter smiled into the darkness. "That's not so old," he said lightly, thinking of his own thirty-nine years.

"I bet that girl feels it though," Hank replied thoughtfully. "She's been through enough to last her a lifetime. I know Otis and Maggie are real worried about her."

"Oh?" Hunter asked casually. He was even more curious about Marilyn than ever now, and he knew that his one word was all the prompting that Hank would need.

"Yes, they're real worried about her. 'Bout six or seven years ago, I forget just when, she married the Davis boy, the one that was a deputy, and they had a baby the year after that. Fine little boy. Well, I guess it was when Bobby was three when Robert—that was her husband—and Bobby went up in the law enforcement helicopter on the Fourth of July, out at the fairgrounds. There was a freak accident and Bobby was killed in the crash. Then the marriage, which Maggie said was shaky to begin with, broke up, and Robert left the state."

"I'm sure she grieved her son terribly," Hunter murmured softly.

"But it's been nearly eighteen months, and she isn't doing as well as Maggie thinks she ought to," Hank protested with real concern in his voice. "Maggie says it's like Marilyn has changed so much. Oh, she seems all right on the outside, but she doesn't see much of her old friends, the ones with little kids, and she flat out won't come back to church anymore. Maggie can't get through to her."

"Well, Hank, people have to work these things through for themselves," Hunter said noncommittally, although his mind was working on the problem.

"Well, I hope she does," Hank said. "There don't seem to be much that anyone else can do," he added sadly as he crushed out his cigarette with his heel and walked back to the reception hall.

Oh, Hank, I don't know about that, Hunter thought as his mind whirled. It was wrong to let a lovely woman like that grieve forever. Life had too much to offer to be spent like that. There's bound to be something that someone can do to help her get over her terrible loss and back to a full life. *And,* Hunter mused, *I might be just the man to do it.*

Marilyn sat in front of the mirror in her small bathroom and brushed her shoulder-length black hair until it was dry, then tied it back off her face and stared at her image critically in the mirror. *It's funny how I can look so alive on the outside and be so close to dead on the inside,* she thought dully. *But I must be more alive than I thought, or this evening would not have hurt me so much.* She stared back at the tanned, oval face in the mirror. It was still pretty enough, even after all she had been through. Even though she would be thirty next month, her face was unlined and her firm features were youthful. Only Marilyn's sad brown eyes gave away her true state. Where once they had sparkled, now they were dull and opaque, dimmed by eighteen months of grieving. *Bobby wouldn't know me these days,* she thought involuntarily as she remembered the smiling "mommy" she once had been.

Willing thoughts of Bobby away, Marilyn stood up and peeled off the bath towel she had wrapped around herself and let it fall to the floor, leaving her naked in full view of the bathroom mirror. She pulled a nightgown out of the bathroom cabinet and started to pull it over her head, then stopped and looked at her body curiously, wondering if it showed any sign of all that had happened in the last six years. No, she concluded, she had exactly the same figure that she had on her wedding night, the same high breasts and narrow waist, the same flat stomach and slim hips, with not so much as a sag or a stretch mark to indicate that she had been pregnant. *It's like he never was,* Marilyn thought sadly as she pulled her gown over her head and turned out the bathroom light. *All I have left of him are his pictures and a whole lot of memories,* she thought despairingly.

That wasn't strictly true, she reminded herself as she wandered into the kitchen for a glass of milk. She still had some of Bobby's clothes and toys packed away in the closet, and his baby furniture was stored in the garage. *It's funny,* she thought, *I have more relics left of the rotten marriage than of my beloved child.* Although she could not wear it since it was much too large for her, out of habit she had left Robert's "Sam Brown," the special belt with bullet loops and a holster that all deputies wore, hanging beside hers in the front closet. Too, she carried his .357 Magnum sometimes when she was on duty, even though it was really too big for her and not as easy to use as her own .38. And she still had the house, even though the payments were a little stiff, and the pickup truck with the oversized cab, which Robert had left behind when he had gone away so abruptly. After the divorce, her family and friends had urged her to sell the truck and buy something smaller, but there was no sense in that, she reasoned. It was a good vehicle and it was paid for. Besides, Bobby had loved riding on the jump seats behind the front seat.

Pouring herself a glass of milk, she found herself thinking about the wedding this evening, even though she had promised herself that she would put the events of tonight out of her mind. Myra was right. The wedding this evening was every bit as lovely as her own had been so many years ago. She had been twenty-four, Robert just a year older, and they had been high-school sweethearts. Robert had put in his stint in the service while she had worked in various offices around New Braunfels. When Robert had gotten out of the service they had gone through deputy training together, and they had both been hired by the county as deputies. They had married in the spring, in the same little church where tonight's wedding had been. Leaving in a cloud of rice and confetti, she and Robert had thought themselves the luckiest couple in the world.

Damn! Marilyn thought as she wandered into the living room and sat down on the couch. It didn't take long for things to sour. Marilyn and Robert had both changed a great deal during Robert's years in the service, and they discovered to their horror that they had nothing basically in common anymore. They realized almost immediately that they had made a serious mistake in their marriage, and were on the verge of separating when Marilyn discovered to her dismay that she was pregnant. Robert offered to stay until the child was born, and then he could not bear to leave his precious son. So the marriage limped along, held together by their mutual love for Robert, Jr., whom they had promptly nicknamed Bobby. Big for his age and sporting a head full of dark curls, Bobby had thoroughly charmed Marilyn and Robert and anyone else who was around him. Marilyn went back to work in the sheriff's office when Bobby was a few months old and she and Robert bought a house, both determined to make a good home for Bobby even if they were not particularly happy as a couple. They were very active in the church, perhaps substituting the rich friendships made there for the emptiness of their own relationship. And then in one cruel instant, Bobby, the light of their lives and the only thing holding them together, was snatched away.

Why did Bobby have to die? Why did I have to lose my baby? she thought for the millionth time as she looked down at the glass of milk that she held in her lap. After the crash, Bobby had been rushed to a San Antonio hospital and they had hoped against hope that he could be saved. But after three days and one operation it was clear that Bobby's brain was dead, and Robert and Marilyn had agreed to the doctors' suggestion that they turn off the life supports. The boy died thirty minutes later, and in a mindless stupor Marilyn had donated his liver to a child who had cancer and who needed a transplant in order to live. Two weeks later, as soon as he was out of the hospital, a grief-stricken Robert packed his belongings and left, sending Marilyn divorce papers a few months later from Yuma, Arizona. Under the circumstances she was almost relieved that Robert had done so. However, she couldn't help adding the feeling of failure in the broken marriage to her grief for Bobby.

Maybe I should have had his funeral in the funeral home, Marilyn thought as she twisted a strand of hair between her fingers. But she had felt that Bobby should be buried from the church where she and Robert had married and where they had worshipped as a family, and not from an impersonal funeral home. Ever since then, the association had been so painful to Marilyn that she had stopped attending services altogether, and she had quietly resigned as the organist. She had requested a transfer from the office to a squad car after the tragedy and now had to work most Sundays, but even on her Sundays off she stayed away from the church, making new friends in the sheriff's department to fill the void left by her defection from the fold. She would have never gone back tonight if Myra hadn't called her and begged her to. After a few months people had begun to drop hints that they had missed her in church, and she had gritted her teeth and changed the subject so often that gossip had spread that she was bitter and that was why she had turned away from the church.

Is it true? Marilyn wondered. *Am I bitter?* Not for the first time, she examined her feelings about the loss of her son. Shocked? Yes. Stunned? Definitely. Grieved? Certainly. But bitter? Not really. At least Marilyn did not think so. She had examined her feelings when she had first heard the gossip, and again on various occasions, and she honestly could not see where she was bitter. She bore no rancor toward the helicopter pilot or Robert, both of whom had miraculously survived the crash, nor did she blame God, although she had asked the anguished question *why?* more than once. *No, I don't think I'm bitter,* she told herself. *I'm just hurt, and it hurts worse inside that church where Bobby spent so many happy hours and where I had to tell him good-bye. I know that's unreasonable, but that is how I feel. That's why I don't want to go back. Because it hurts so much to go.*

Sighing, Marilyn carried her half-empty milk glass into the kitchen and poured it into the sink. Unbidden, the piercing eyes of Hunter Templeton came to her mind, and she remembered the way he had asked her to play for his services and then offered her his handkerchief when she needed it. *I bet he's curious now,* she thought suddenly, *and he'll go find one of the local gossips and find out about me. And then he'll feel obligated to help.*

Bristling at the thought, Marilyn snapped off the kitchen light and padded to the bedroom, where she climbed under the sheets and stared up at the ceiling, eerily patterned by the moonlight shining through the branches of the oak tree outside the window. As hard as she tried, she could not put Hunter Templeton out of her mind.

He would be coming around, of that she was sure. She had seen him eyeing her curiously at the reception and he would probably seek out someone like Hank Schriever and find out about the tragedy. Hank would fill the minister's ear with the sad tale of poor Marilyn Davis, and can anyone do anything to get the lonely girl back in church where she belongs? *Why can't people just leave me alone?* she thought disgustedly. Now that she had unwittingly sparked his interest, Hunter would probably try to do his bit for the poor, grieving mother. *Yes, try to do his Christian duty by me. He'll come up with some ploy or another to get me back into the church. Well, maybe I'll forgo the polite route and just tell him to get lost,* she thought as she turned over and curled her arm around her pillow. No, she couldn't do that. He had been too kind to her this evening. *But I do prefer to be left alone and I'll simply tell him so,* she vowed, and hoped that Hunter would take the hint and leave her alone. With that thought in mind, Marilyn drifted into slumber, going to sleep without tears in her eyes for the first time in over a year.

CHAPTER TWO

Wurstfest gets more crowded by the year, thought Marilyn as she pushed her beige western hat up a little and surveyed the crowd with a professional eye, looking out for anything amiss. So far, everything was calm, but then it was early in the evening yet. The two Saturday nights of the ten-day festival were the busiest, and Marilyn and the other deputies were just a little more cautious on Saturday. Not that anything serious had ever happened, Marilyn thought as she sniffed the air, enjoying the rich, tangy smell of the various local sausages from which *Wurstfest* got its name. In fact, working *Wurstfest* was almost fun if you didn't mind lots of people, lots of sausage, and lots of beer. Started some years ago as a strictly local party, *Wurstfest* had soon become known all over south central Texas as a delightful way to spend an evening or two, and tourists flocked in for the day from all over south Texas, coming in droves from San Antonio and Austin. In fact, the university in San Marcos, just a few miles away, could have supported *Wurstfest* singlehandedly if it had to.

Marilyn wandered over to a soft-drink booth and purchased a Coke, then sat for a moment to rest her tired feet before she resumed her patrol. She sipped her Coke and surveyed the booth pavilion that was as large as a city block and housed every kind of booth imaginable. Besides the inevitable bratwurst, knackwurst, and frankfurter stands, there were booths selling rich, delicate apple strudel and other German pastries, delicate potato pancakes, and thick slabs of roast beef. Other booths sold Tyrolean hats and other souvenirs of the old country, T-shirts with WURSTFEST emblazoned across them proudly, and buttons that proclaimed KISS ME, I'M GERMAN. In one corner a skillful caricature artist plied his trade, and at either end of the pavilion a busy beer concession slaked the thirst of the hungry crowd.

Amused, Marilyn watched three hungry college boys with Southwest Texas State sweat shirts consume their bratwursts-on-a-bun in two bites, then chase it down with a hefty swig of beer. *I hope they follow that with more food,* Marilyn thought, *if they intend to drive back to San Marcos tonight.* One of the boys caught her eye and smiled sheepishly at her, as though he knew what she was thinking and was trying to reassure her of his intent. *He wouldn't have cared what I thought if I didn't have on this uniform,* Marilyn thought with amusement as the boys wandered toward another food booth. *It's amazing how much difference the uniform makes,* she mused, not for the first time. Without it, she was just another attractive young woman, and people regarded her as that and no more. But when she donned the brown pants, beige shirt, boots, Sam Brown, and badge, she suddenly became the voice of authority, and the law-abiding people that she usually dealt with treated her as such.

Marilyn finished her Coke and crumpled the paper cup in her hand, then searched out a garbage can in which to put it. Admitting to herself that she probably would have thrown it down if she hadn't been in uniform, she smiled sardonically at her attitude as she tossed the cup into an already-overflowing garbage barrel and resumed her patrol.

As she left the food pavilion, the face of Hunter Templeton floated across her mind and she wondered with surprise what on earth had made her think of him. She had not given him more than a thought or two all day, keeping her promise to herself not to think about last night's painful experience at the wedding. Besides, *Wurstfest* was the last place that a minister was likely to go, especially on Saturday night. Although *Wurstfest* was wonderful fun, it did tend to get a little wild as the night wore on and the beer flowed freely.

"Hey, Marilyn, wait up a minute," Tess Hamilton called across the walkway as she strode through the crowd. "Just want to say hi. I haven't seen you in what? Two weeks?"

"At least that long," Marilyn said as she grasped Tess's hand. Tess was a reserve deputy who taught high-school English, one of the many deputies who had other daytime jobs and who worked on weekends and holidays when the force needed extra people. She was one of the best reserve deputies on the force, and Marilyn considered her a close friend as well. They had shared many a cup of coffee together after a long shift, and Marilyn was a frequent visitor in Tess's noisy, happy home. "You haven't been working much, have you?" Marilyn asked as Tess fell into step beside her. "You haven't been on my shift."

"No, I cut back for a few weeks," Tess admitted. "Jimmy's starting quarterback for the football team this year," she said with a grin. "Once football season is over, though, I'll be back on just as often as they'll use me. We'll have three in college next year and I need the money."

"That's great," Marilyn said, smiling. *I wish I could have had that problem someday,* she thought with a pang. A disturbance caught the corner of her eye and she nudged Tess with her elbow, all personal thoughts forgotten. "Over there, Tess. I think we may have a problem."

"Yep," Tess nodded as they headed toward the fence that surrounded the *Wurstfest* grounds. "Looks like Godzilla there had a little too much of the good brew."

He must weigh two seventy-five, Marilyn thought in despair as she stared up at the sodden redhead sprawled against the fence, snoring softly. *How are we going to get* him to the trailer? Marilyn and her fellow deputies were not overly zealous about enforcing the public intoxication law, figuring that if a person could conduct himself with a reasonable amount of decorum, then he was not intoxicated, but this fellow was clearly not just intoxicated, but drunk as a skunk. "I guess we better take him in," Marilyn said doubtfully.

"And how do you propose to do that?" Tess asked cynically. "They don't issue us wheelbarrows." She looked up at the drunk with a disgusted eye. "He must have been at it all afternoon to be in this shape."

Marilyn reached up on her tiptoes and sniffed his breath, gagging when the drunk opened his mouth and burped right in her face. "Whiskey and gin," she informed Tess as she stepped back, taking off her hat to fan her face a little. "He didn't get that kind of booze here on the grounds."

"But he got himself here, didn't he?" Tess grumbled as she eyed the man. "Now, how do we get him out?"

"Officers, may I be of some assistance?" a deep, familiar voice asked at Marilyn's elbow.

"Reverend Templeton!" Marilyn exclaimed as she whirled around and stared with astonishment at the minister. What was he doing at *Wurstfest?*

"Mrs. Davis!" Hunter replied, almost as surprised as Marilyn. "I didn't recognize you in the uniform with your hair up."

"Yes, it does make a difference," Marilyn admitted. This was not the first time that an acquaintance had failed to recognize her in uniform. Not that Hunter looked the same as he had last night either, for that matter, she thought. Tonight he had gotten rid of the dark suit that he had been wearing last night, and was dressed in a pair of faded jeans and a tight short-sleeved knit shirt that showed off every muscle in his chest and arms and revealed a small tattoo on his left arm above his elbow. Marilyn's mouth went dry as she noted the rippling perfection of the upper part of his body, and she wondered momentarily what he would look like with his shirt off. When she realized what she was thinking, she turned her head back to the drunk in order to hide the telltale flush that spread up her face. For heaven's sake, what was she thinking of? She couldn't feel *that* way about him! He was the minister. Although she had never put ministers up on the pedestal that many people did, she had never thought of a minister as an exciting man either, and the knowledge that she thought of Hunter in that way embarrassed her thoroughly.

At that precise moment the giant drunk woke up. He stared at Marilyn for a bleary moment, then his foggy gaze left her and found Tess. "Lady cops!" he crowed as he lurched forward and stumbled a little. His massive legs turned to rubber, and he swayed a little and sank to the ground, where he leaned against the fence and stared at the women in sodden astonishment. "Purty lady cops," he added as he laid his head back and snored loudly.

Marilyn whirled around and bit her lip, trying not to laugh, but she glimpsed Tess's crinkling face and a bubble of mirth escaped her, then another, and the two women stood laughing at the man, grateful for the shadows that hid them from the crowd. Marilyn looked up and was surprised to find Hunter laughing so hard that tears were running down his face. "You know, we're terrible," he gasped.

"Yes, I know," Marilyn said as fresh waves of laughter rippled from her throat. "I have to arrest him, and you ought to be praying for him, and all we can do is stand around and laugh!"

"Pray for him?" Tess asked in astonishment. "Don't tell me you're the new minister!"

"Hunter Templeton," he said, extending his hand to Tess.

"Well, I'll be," Tess said as she took his hand. "Glad to meet you, Reverend Templeton. Father Donovan said that your church and ours are planning to head up the Christmas food drive together this year." She gazed at Hunter with glazed admiration in her expression.

Oh, good grief, Marilyn thought as she caught the expression on her friend's face. *Tess, aren't you a little old for that?* But in all honesty, Tess probably was not more than a few years older than Hunter, and what was the harm in looking? Still, it made Marilyn distinctly uneasy to see her friend openly admiring Hunter, although she couldn't for the life of her figure out why she should care.

The drunken man burped in his sleep. "I really don't think he's going to resist arrest, but getting him to the trailer is going to take some work," Tess said as her eyes reluctantly left Hunter. "I'll go get a couple of the men and we can carry him in."

Marilyn nodded. "Try to find Joe Ramirez. He's nice and big and ought to be able to handle this idiot."

"No need for that, Mrs. Davis," Hunter said easily as he knelt down beside the snoring man. "If you two can get his other shoulder, I think we should be able to walk him in." He knelt and slid his arm around the drunk, lifting him to his feet. The huge man immediately started to slide back down.

"Come on, buddy, you're under arrest. Anything you say can and may be used in court against you," Marilyn said as she grabbed his other shoulder and hoisted the man upward. It was no good. The man was so far gone that his legs simply would not support him.

"Let me get his feet," Tess volunteered as she grasped his huge ankles in her arms. "Okay, heave him up and let's go!"

"I'll read him his rights at the trailer," Marilyn muttered as she lent her support to his other shoulder. Together they propped the man up and started for the trailer.

The walk to the trailer was unending. Not only was the man horribly heavy, but it was unbelievably awkward trying to fight their way through the thickening crowd. People pointed and laughed and made catcalls until Marilyn wanted to die of embarrassment. Then, to make matters worse, the man roused up enough to start singing "Anchors Away" at the top of his lungs. They reached the law enforcement trailer just as Marilyn thought her shoulder and arm were about to fall off. They stopped halfway up the steps, and Tess let go of one leg and banged on the door.

"What the hell you got there, girls?" Boyd Lewis boomed in his gravelly bass voice as he threw open the door. "Oh, it's a sumbitchin' drunk. Well, bring him on in." Boyd turned around and, in his usual salty language, instructed a couple of the younger deputies to come and give them a hand.

Gratefully Marilyn relinquished her singing burden and rubbed her shoulder. She was going to be sore in the morning. That man had been heavy! Hesitant, she turned to Hunter and caught him rubbing his shoulder too. He must have supported most of the man's weight, Marilyn realized. "Thank you for the help," she said softly. "We'd still be out there with him if you hadn't happened along."

"No problem," Hunter replied easily. He put his hand in the small of her back and gently pushed her into the trailer, stepping in behind her and pulling shut the door. Inside was the usual clutter of desks and chairs, with portable facilities for crowd control and arrests. The other deputies had already begun processing the drunk to the best of their ability, which was somewhat hampered by the fact that the man had gone back to sleep and was not able to answer any of their questions.

Marilyn sat down and began filling out the report that always accompanied an arrest, and tried to stifle the embarrassment that was growing with every moment that Hunter spent in the trailer. The other deputies obviously did not realize that Hunter was a minister, since they were filling the air with their usual blue conversation. Marilyn had become inured to it during her years on the force and had been known to use it on occasion herself, but she grew more horrified every minute that Hunter stood there. Why was he waiting around? It would be all right for him to leave now if he wanted to.

"Marilyn, are you through with those damn papers yet?" Boyd boomed across the room. "Sleeping Beauty needs his picture taken."

"Nearly finished, Boyd," she replied as she stepped in front of the camera. The deputies always took their picture with anyone they arrested so that they could later identify the person in court if they had to. Marilyn stood patiently while the young deputies carried the drunk over to the camera and propped him beside Marilyn.

"Hold his damn head up!" Doyd snarled as the man's head drooped onto his chest.

Marilyn reached out and grasped his hair and yanked his head up, holding it long enough for Boyd to take the picture. That done, she left him to the tender mercies of the paddy wagon and headed for the door, picking her hat up from the table. She turned and saw Hunter start to follow her out the door. "Thank you again for the help," she said.

"Yes, thanks a damn lot for the help," Boyd boomed in Hunter's ear. "Always nice when a citizen will come forward like that. Damn nice. By the way, I didn't get your name."

"Hunter Templeton," he replied softly.

It took a minute for the name to register with Boyd. "The new minister?" he asked sheepishly. Hunter nodded. "Like I said," Boyd stammered, turning a bright shade of red, "very nice of you to help."

"I'm sorry about the language," Marilyn said as they shut the door and walked down the steps. "They talk like that all the time."

Hunter laughed. "I heard, and used, worse than that in the navy. Still, they shouldn't use it in front of a lady."

"What lady?" Marilyn asked, puzzled. "Oh, me? I'm no lady. I'm a deputy."

"Could have fooled me," Hunter murmured as he surveyed her long slender body, her curves not entirely hidden by the uniform. A telltale blush crept up Marilyn's cheeks and she wondered what Hunter was thinking. Surely he wasn't noticing her as a woman! Yet, she had to admit that she definitely saw him as a man. *No*, she thought. *I don't want to feel like that toward him—Toward any man.*

"I better resume patrol," she said as Hunter took her arm. "Thank you again. I'll see you sometime soon."

"Just a moment," Hunter said smoothly as he took her arm and steered her in the opposite direction from her patrol. "I think you earned your money tonight, and what I have to ask won't take but a minute."

"Reverend Templeton, I really must get back on patrol," Marilyn began as she tried to turn around, but his hand gripped her arm firmly, and short of making a scene she had to go with him. *Here it comes*, she thought. *Just like I expected. The good deed. I wonder what he's come up with?* Unconsciously her mouth set in a firm, hard line. *Whatever he wants I'll turn him down as politely as I know how*, she vowed.

"I thought it would take me hours to find you," Hunter

admitted as he found a deserted bench in a corner of the grounds that was not too crowded. "I never dreamed it would be so easy," he added.

So he had come to *Wurstfest* especially to find her! *He must really want to do me a favor,* Marilyn thought cynically.

"I believe you had something you wanted to ask me?" Marilyn prompted him coolly.

Hunter's face froze into an expressionless mask when he saw the cool look on hers. "Yes, I have a big favor to ask. You're working the evening shift this week, right?"

"Yes," Marilyn replied shortly.

"Then you're free in the morning?" he added.

"More or less," she said quietly.

"Then would you be able to play for services tomorrow? Mrs. Weissmann is ill and . . ."

"Please, no, Reverend Templeton!" Marilyn said quickly. "I just don't want to do it. It makes me miserable to go back in that church where I buried my child, and I don't want to put myself through that."

"I know that, and Mrs. Weissmann knows that," Hunter said slowly. "But we thought that under the circumstances . . ."

"What circumstances?" Marilyn asked suspiciously. "I'm sure you've found out all about me and have decided to do me a favor, but this isn't the first time somebody's cooked up some scheme to get poor grieving Marilyn back in the fold. What did you do, cook up a little head cold for her? Or maybe a touch of arthritis?"

"No, as a matter of fact we cooked up a compound fracture of her left arm," Hunter replied, angry now and not bothering to hide it. "Complete with a hospital stay and traction. All for you. Just to do a good deed for poor Marilyn Davis."

Marilyn turned first red then pale as the impact of his

words sunk in. "I'm sorry," she whispered. "I didn't know she was really hurt. How bad is it?" she asked anxiously. Mrs. Weissmann had taught her to play the organ and Marilyn loved the old lady dearly.

"Pretty bad," Hunter replied sternly. "She'll be in the hospital for a good two weeks and out of commission for another month after that. And instead of worrying about herself, she's laying there fretting about church tomorrow. She needs your help and so do I. Right now I couldn't care less how you feel about the church or about doing a good deed for you. I just desperately need an organist, and I'd like to be able to assure Mrs. Weissmann that her beloved services are taken care of."

"I'm sorry I thought what I did," Marilyn replied, close to tears. "But I simply won't go back there. It tears me apart. Look, I damn near caved in when my boy died and Robert left, but I've put myself back together and I've gone on by eliminating those things from my life that make me remember. I'm sorry, but the church does that to me."

"I know how you feel," Hunter replied. "All right, so maybe I don't," he amended as she looked at him unbelievingly. "All I know is that the church should be the place you turn to, not away from, with your grief." His eyes narrowed and he looked at her searchingly with his piercing black eyes. "Look, you're not the first or the last who has had to rebuild a life after a tragedy, and from what I've seen, those who do it in the church do a better job of it than those who turn away. But tonight that's beside the point. I just need you to play for me. Mrs. Weissmann needs you," he added firmly.

Marilyn shook her head. "I just don't know," she said haltingly. "Can I call you after I get off my shift?"

"I need to know one way or the other now," Hunter replied heavily. "If you won't do it, I'll have to call Father

Donovan and see if they have an extra organist over there, or else bring in a piano for Susan Thomas to play."

"All right, all right, I'll play for you," Marilyn replied, throwing up her hands in surrender. "Is Brad Thomas still the director? Tell him that I'll be there by ten fifteen to go over the special music with him. And what are you preaching on?"

"The peace of God. Why?" Hunter asked.

"So I won't play 'Onward Christian Soldiers' for an offertory," Marilyn replied dryly. As she realized what she had committed herself to, a numbing apprehension gripped her and her face paled. "I don't think I can do it," she said weakly. "What if I don't make it through the service? I almost didn't get through the wedding last night without breaking down in tears."

Hunter reached out and ran his hand down the side of her face. "Yes, you can to it, Marilyn," he said firmly. "I'll pray for you," he added softly as he turned and walked away.

Marilyn ran her hand down the side of her face where Hunter had touched her and stared into the crowd long after Hunter had been swallowed up into it. What had she just committed herself to? After over a year of resistance, he had worn her down in about fifteen minutes! Where had her resolve gone? *But I couldn't let Mrs. Weissmann down,* she reminded herself firmly. *I'm doing it for her, not Hunter Templeton.* But she wasn't, not really, and she knew it. And she wasn't doing it out of the goodness of her heart, she knew that too. *It's him,* she thought. *I'm doing it for Hunter.* Even though she didn't want to be, she was attracted to the virile minister. *But I can't be,* she told herself. *I don't want to be! That part of my life left with Robert.*

Oh, no, it didn't, a little voice in her head chided her. The only thing that had left was Robert himself!

* * *

Marilyn walked up the stone steps and entered the sanctuary slowly, pulling the thick wooden door to shut out the brisk wind. Although the sun was warm, a chilly autumn wind blew through the branches of the trees outside and slipped into every crack and open space in the old church. A momentary memory of the sanctuary filled with funeral flowers flashed into her mind, but she quickly banished the thought and concentrated on the church as it appeared this morning. Brad Thomas, the choir director, and a few of the choir were waiting for her, but apparently most of the choir members were either in Sunday school or had not arrived yet. Marilyn forced herself to stop trembling and strode down the wide aisle and stepped up to the organ, noticing idly that a large flower arrangement from the wedding adorned the altar. Briskly, so as not to give herself time to think, Marilyn stepped up on the platform and switched on the organ. "What are you singing this morning?" she asked.

"I don't know if you know this one, Marilyn," Brad replied as he handed her a copy of the sheet music. "It came out just a year ago."

Marilyn took the music and flipped through it. She had never seen it before, but as she scanned the music quickly she realized that it was a simple though lovely piece to play. "Take me through it, Brad," she said as she quickly set up the stops, tested them for balance by playing a few chords, and took out a little of the brass. Brad conducted her through the simple anthem, telling her as she went how loud or soft he wanted it, and when to retard. "How was it?" she asked as she finished her last chord.

"Fine, but could you take out a little more brass?" Brad asked, grinning a little.

"Right, don't want to bowl them over," Marilyn said as

she pushed in the offending stops. They went over the piece again, this time with the choir.

Brad came around the organ and hugged Marilyn tightly. "It's sure good to have you back," he said softly. Brad had never made a secret of the fact that he admired Marilyn, and after the divorce he had called her a few times to go out. She had refused him and he had since married, but his sincere delight in seeing Marilyn again brought stinging tears to the back of her eyes.

"I'm playing for only a few weeks, until Mrs. Weissmann is able to take over," she replied softly.

Brad's face fell. "Well, we'll enjoy the next few weeks then," he replied gamely.

They went over the anthem once again with the choir, then the choir members retired to the robing room and Marilyn opened her book of organ solos and propped it at her favorite offertory. It was a quiet transcription of a beloved old hymn, and it had been her favorite in the old days. At first with cautious fingers, and then more surely as the music flowed from her, Marilyn played the lovely old piece, letting the melody move from her heart through her fingers into the organ. She was trembling when she finished, not from fear, but from an emotion that she could not define, nor did she want to. She just wanted to let the music flow from her again, as it had so often in years past.

"That was lovely," Hunter said softly as Marilyn marked the spot in her book with a bulletin.

"Thank you," she said simply and sincerely. This morning Hunter was dressed in a suit again, but she could not quite banish the vision of him as he had looked in the tight shirt and jeans at *Wurstfest,* or forget the attraction she had felt for him dressed that way. She looked at her watch and then at Hunter. "Reverend Templeton, I don't mean to be impertinent, but the service starts in twenty minutes.

Shouldn't you be getting into your robe?" She had better go and find hers.

"I don't preach in a robe," Hunter replied easily, glancing down at his gray pinstripe suit. "I feel that it puts me up on a pedestal. I'd rather my congregation thought of me as one of them."

"Oh," Marilyn said, pleased that Hunter felt the way he did about his congregation. "Well, unlike you, I do wear a robe, and I better go and find it before I have to start the prelude."

She slid off the bench and ducked quickly into the robing room, where she found her special robe with banded sleeves hanging just where she had left it the last time she had worn it, the Sunday before the tragedy. It was covered with a cleaning bag and obviously had not been worn by anyone else. *They were keeping it for me,* Marilyn thought as she removed the plastic cover and stepped into the robe, tears stinging her eyes. Touched by the expression of loyalty, she sniffed and slipped into the bathroom, which was mercifully deserted, and blew her nose vigorously into a paper towel.

A number of people were already seated in the sanctuary when Marilyn returned to the platform. She ignored the muted whispers that spread through the congregation like a prairie fire and sat down to the organ. She opened a book of simple prelude pieces and selected one that she could play with no practice, going over and over it as the sanctuary filled. Adjusting the volume as the noise level grew, she concentrated on playing and blocked out the whispers of the congregation, some of which she knew were about her. Determinedly she thrust aside her ragged emotions and her confused feelings about being back in this church and let the sweet sounds of holy music pervade her consciousness to the exclusion of all else. When Brad gave the signal, she automatically went into the call to worship, playing it softly until the choir and then Hunter had filed in, then allowed the volume to swell as Brad signaled for the congregation to stand. The majestic strains stirred Marilyn's heart as she responded to the call to worship.

After the congregational singing, Hunter rose to greet the guests and make the usual announcements regarding the coming week's activities. Although he did mention Mrs. Weissmann's accident, mercifully he did not draw attention to Marilyn by publicly thanking her for stepping in. From the organ Marilyn was looking at Hunter's right side, and even at that angle he seemed to fit behind the pulpit. *I was wrong about him,* she thought. *He does seem like a preacher; at least when he's up there he does.*

Marilyn surreptitiously got out her offertory and propped it up as the ushers came forward with the offering plates. As she scanned the lines of music, as she sometimes did during the offertory prayer, nervous perspiration filmed her upper lip, and she had to wipe her hands on her robe. *Oh, no, I can't go through with it,* she thought suddenly. *Bobby used to sit on the bench beside me while I practiced this. This was his favorite. Why didn't I pick something else?* Terrified, she gasped softly. Hunter looked up for a moment from Hank Schriever's prayer and nodded encouragingly, as though he knew that she was upset, then closed his eyes again. Suddenly Marilyn was calm. She didn't understand the effect Hunter had on her, and right now she couldn't analyze it, but she was grateful for it. She had to play in a moment, and his comforting nod had made all the difference.

Hank's resounding "Amen" rang through the church as Marilyn's cue. Whispering a short "Lord, help me," she laid her hands on the keys and began to play. Almost immediately she was caught up in the rapture of the beautiful, quiet piece, forgetting her sorrow, totally oblivious to the effect that the stirring old melody was having on the others. As she played she could feel peace flooding her heart, peace that she had not known in a very long time. It would not last, she knew; her grief would come back to haunt her, but for now she would savor the feeling.

She ended the music just as the ushers retired from the auditorium, and turned to get out the special music, then stared in astonishment at the congregation. They were sitting silent, rapt, tears flowing down many of the women's faces. Her eyes flew to Hunter's, and even in his eyes there was a suspicion of moisture. Suddenly profoundly moved by the emotions she had so eloquently expressed on the keyboard, Marilyn's own eyes began to fill, and she wiped them quickly with the sleeve of her robe as she opened the special music. The choir sang beautifully, perhaps inspired by her and, suddenly exhausted by the emotions of the morning, Marilyn slid off the organ bench gratefully and took her customary place on the front pew as Hunter rose to speak.

Hunter was not a fire-breathing preacher of the old school. Far from it. Yet, as he spoke, quietly and gravely, he captured Marilyn's attention as no hellfire and brimstone speaker could have ever done. He spoke of peace, the peace of the world as opposed to the peace of God. The two were not one and the same, he said, explaining the difference. He went on to say that even though man's problems in the world almost always prevented worldly peace, that with God a man could always find the inner peace for which he longed, no matter what his outward circumstances. He used both Biblical and contemporary examples to illustrate and strengthen his point. It was almost as though he were speaking to Marilyn personally, assuring her that her sore heart could have the peace for which it longed. *Oh, I hope you're right,* she thought. *I hope you're right.*

Deeply moved by Hunter's stirring message, she played the last anthem with trembling fingers, then escaped to the robing room and shed her robe quickly, answering the inevitable greetings of welcome from the choir with a weak nod. Hoping to escape to her car, she was waylaid by Brad Thomas and dragged to the foyer, where it seemed like everyone in the little church had waited to speak to her. "We're so glad to have you back!" they said over and over. "It was so wonderful to hear you play!" "Will you play for us often?" Emotionally exhausted, Marilyn greeted her old friends as best she could and said that she would play for them again.

At the other end of the foyer Hunter was greeting the churchgoers warmly, asking about those absent because of illness and chatting for a moment or two with each family. Finally the crowd began to thin and Marilyn slipped out the door before Hunter could speak to her. As she fled to her car, the inevitable stragglers greeted her with the same delight that she had found inside the church, and she had to visit with them for a moment also. Finally, escaping to her truck, she sat alone until the lot cleared, then drove the short block to the cemetery and parked along the curb. Pushing open the gate, she walked inside and headed automatically for the little grave marker on the far side of the grounds.

Marilyn was not normally one to visit the cemetery. She usually brought flowers on Christmas and on the anniversary of the tragedy, and that was all. But today she needed to come, although she was not completely sure why. She knew that she had been through a trying but healing experience, and she needed to be close to her little one, even if he didn't know she was there. She stood, not speaking, as the emotional strain of the morning gave way to harsh sobs. For long minutes she cried, healing tears streaming down her face.

Hunter locked the church and climbed into his car. He had been a little worried about Marilyn Davis, but she had been fine. She had played as movingly as he had ever heard anyone, professional or amateur, play an organ, then greeted her old friends warmly. Pulling out of the driveway, he noticed a big yellow pickup parked at the cemetery gate and turned his own car in that direction instead of toward the parsonage. He drove by slowly, identifying the truck as hers, and spotting the lonely figure standing in front of the little stone, her head bent. *So she didn't do as well as I thought she had,* he mused. It really hurt her to come back, even though she needed to come. Hunter wondered for a moment if there was anything he could do for her at this point, then turned his car around and drove toward the parsonage.

Marilyn pushed away her half-eaten peanut butter sandwich and listlessly sipped her iced tea. It was barely one in the afternoon, almost four hours before she had to report for duty. Thank goodness she was working *Wurstfest* again and had that to keep her mind off her turbulent emotions. No, she was not sorry that she had played for the services, painful as it had been. Despite the inevitable memories, she had thrilled at making music like that again. She had missed her music since the tragedy. Even though she sometimes played at home, it simply was not the same. Maybe this morning was the beginning of the healing of her spirit, and although it had left her spent emotionally, it had done her a world of good. Hunter had been right in wanting her to come and play. She did need to be back in church, and she needed to make music again. Exhausted by the morning, she laid down on the couch and stared at the ceiling, wishing she could go to sleep but knowing that she wouldn't.

Marilyn jumped at the sound of knuckles sharply rapping on her front door. She peeked out of the window and was astonished to find Hunter Templeton standing on her front porch with his hands in his pockets. Slowly she unlatched the front door and stared out of it, conscious of the tear stains that had dried on her cheeks. "Hello, Reverend Templeton," she said softly.

Hunter looked at her quickly, not missing the pale cheeks or her red eyes. "I just wanted to thank you for coming this morning," he said as Marilyn moved to let him enter. His big frame seemed to fill Marilyn's small living room. "Are you all right?" he asked softly.

Marilyn shrugged. "I think so," she said. "As for this morning, don't worry about it. I was glad to do it."

"That's a lie, and you know it," Hunter replied, a soft smile taking the sting out of his words. "That was very hard for you, and I'm sure my attitude last night didn't help you one bit."

"You were also right—I needed to go back," Marilyn said dryly. "I said it's all right, and it is."

"So I take that to mean that you'll be back next Sunday?" Hunter asked.

"Is that why you came all the way over here?" Marilyn asked shrewdly. "Yes, I'll play for you next Sunday."

"As a matter of fact, that isn't why I came, although I don't mind hearing that you'll be back," Hunter replied honestly. "I came to offer you an afternoon at the ice cream parlor. Sunday afternoon just isn't Sunday afternoon without a double dip of fresh cherry ice cream."

"Well, I don't know," Marilyn hesitated. She was emotionally wrung out, and she wouldn't be very good company. And why was Hunter Templeton asking her for ice cream? Did he want something else from her? Or was he just doing his Christian duty by a lonely member of the congregation?

"Marilyn, I'm lonely," Hunter said suddenly. "Aren't you?"

"Yes," she replied frankly. She was lonely, and it would be better, infinitely better, to spend the afternoon with Hunter than to spend it alone, brooding. And if he was as lonely as she was, then he wasn't asking her out just to be nice. "I'll go on one condition," she said, a soft smile playing around her lips.

"What's that?" Hunter asked a little warily.

"I get a triple dip of butter pecan," she replied triumphantly. "Let me wash my face, and I'll be ready to go."

CHAPTER THREE

"Where's your car?" Marilyn asked as she and Hunter walked down her sidewalk toward the street.

"I walked over," Hunter replied easily. "I felt so cooped up in that house that I just had to get out and stretch my legs a little. I guess we can go in your truck, if that's all right."

"Sure, Reverend Templeton," Marilyn replied, fishing around in her purse for the keys, fumbling around in vain to find the jingling ring.

"Make it Hunter," he replied easily as he reached down into her messy purse and triumphantly held up the keys.

"How did you do that?" Marilyn asked in wonder, looking at her keys. "I couldn't call you Hunter," she protested with embarrassment.

"Why not?" Hunter replied. "I'm going to call you by your first name. I don't stand on ceremony; why should you?"

"I guess you're right, Rev—Hunter," she said as they climbed into the truck. Marilyn started the engine and backed out of the driveway. "Where to?" she asked.

"Wherever we can get the best ice cream in New Braunfels," he replied.

"Okay," she replied. "There's a little place where they serve mostly homemade ice cream that is out of this world," she volunteered, suddenly remembering the way Bobby had loved the chocolate, and wincing a little.

Hunter noticed the grimace. "We can go somewhere else if you prefer," he said gently.

"No, this one is fine," she replied resolutely. She turned

onto one of the main thoroughfares and headed for downtown.

Hunter ran his hand down the upholstery of the truck. "This is a nice truck, but isn't it a little big for just you?" he asked.

Marilyn shrugged. "It was Robert's," she said matter-of-factly. "He didn't want it when he left. I really enjoyed your sermon this morning," she added smoothly. "Does it take you a long time to prepare a message like that?"

Hunter looked at her sharply, realizing that she was changing the subject, but letting it go without further probing. "This morning's sermon, no. That kind of message needs to be preached, and preached often, with the world the way it is, and people having to cope with the various facets of modern life. For that kind of message I have a file of scripture references, clippings, and so forth that I can turn to. After consulting with my Heavenly Boss"—Hunter grinned and winked broadly—"I sit down and pull the ideas that seem most relevant to the particular congregation that I'm speaking to. In just a few hours it's ready. Now, if I'm covering a more esoteric topic, or a controversial one, I might spend several days researching the topic in my reference books before I even come up with an outline."

"That's lots of work," Marilyn admitted as she parked in front of the ice cream parlor. The little shop had old-fashioned ice cream chairs and a striped awning much like the one that it had sported fifty years ago when it opened. "Here we are," she said unnecessarily.

"This is nice," Hunter murmured. "Do you come here often?"

"I used to," Marilyn admitted. "Not anymore." She climbed out of the truck and closed the door behind her.

Hunter joined her on the sidewalk and together they entered the little shop. The pretty teenage girl at the counter had a bright smile for them both, greeting Hunter as Reverend Templeton and telling him shyly that she liked his sermon. "And I liked the way you played this morning," she added to Marilyn. "Mom and Dad said that having you back was great."

Suddenly the girl's eyes flew open wide as she realized that Hunter and Marilyn were on what could be construed as a date. *Uh-oh,* Marilyn thought, *Hunter and I are going to be the topic of at least one dinner-table conversation tonight!* Shrugging, she looked over the tubs of brightly colored ice cream but settled on her old favorite, butter pecan. She protested, but Hunter insisted on ordering her a triple-dip cone, and instead of the fresh cherry that he had raved about, he ordered a hot fudge sundae.

"Hunter, I'm never going to be able to finish this," Marilyn complained as they sat down at one of the tables with their treat. Hunter took the plastic spoon and dug into the sundae.

"Well, I can finish mine," he replied as he came up with a spoonful of cold ice cream and dripping fudge. "This is lunch."

"Why didn't you say so?" Marilyn asked accusingly. "I would have fixed you something at my house! I guess preachers really don't get fed by a member of the congregation every Sunday, do they?"

"Nope," Hunter replied, taking another luscious bite. "And I'm really a lousy cook. I've learned to do pretty much everything else as a bachelor, but I'm afraid that I just can't get past broiling steaks and opening cans."

Curious, Marilyn nibbled the first dip of her ice cream cone and cocked her head. "Have you ever been married?" she asked.

"Sure haven't," Hunter replied easily. "And before you get that funny little look on your face like everybody gets, yes, I have the normal instincts."

47

"Oh, I knew *that*," Marilyn said frankly, then blushed to the roots of her hair when she realized what she had said. "I—I mean-well . . ."

"Thank you for the vote of confidence," Hunter said dryly, deepening Marilyn's blush.

"Never met the right woman yet?" Marilyn asked perceptively.

Hunter nodded his head. "I thought I had met her once, but when I decided to become a minister, she backed out. I almost gave up the ministry to marry her, but I just felt too compelled to become a preacher. Since then there just hasn't been anyone else."

He must have a tremendous faith, Marilyn thought, *to give up a fiancée over it. More than I'll ever have.* She looked at the arm with the tattoo and a frown of concentration crossed her face. "How did you ever decide to become a minister?" Marilyn asked suddenly, as the question popped into her mind. "I mean, you don't seem much like someone who would . . ." Embarrassed, she trailed off miserably.

"Ah-ha! You don't think I look like a preacher!" he said accusingly, shaking his finger at her.

"No, you don't," Marilyn replied with spirit, taking a bite out of the second dip in her cone.

"And you don't look like a deputy either," he replied. "So I'll tell you how I ended up a preacher if you'll tell me how you ended up a deputy."

"All right," Marilyn laughed. "You first."

Hunter stopped laughing and his face became suddenly serious. "My parents had very strong religious beliefs and they shared those beliefs with me at a very early age. I was no saint, of course," he said, grinning wickedly, "but I always felt that I had a purpose on earth and the hope that it wouldn't be all over when I died. I was secure in that." Hunter stopped and rubbed the space between his eyes.

"Then I went into the navy, intending to make a career of it." He grinned and patted the tattoo on his arm. "Right away, of course, I got shipped to Vietnam. We were stationed on the coast, not in the worst of it, but we saw plenty of action and I got to watch my fellow sailors up close as they tried to cope with both living and dying. And, Marilyn, they just couldn't. Half of them couldn't find a purpose in living, and almost none of them who had to could face dying. That shook me, watching men plead with the Almighty to spare them because they were afraid to die. So I came back and went to college and the seminary, and now I try to help people learn to deal with and live fully the life they have here and prepare with anticipation for the next one."

Marilyn nodded wordlessly. That had been her only consolation for the last eighteen months, the strong feeling that Bobby had gone on to something else.

"And if I can teach them to be more decent individuals while they are here, then so much the better!" Hunter added wickedly.

They both laughed. "You don't think, then, that your primary responsibility is to help people become better?" Marilyn asked curiously. "Some ministers seem to feel that way."

"Well, yes and no," Hunter said thoughtfully. "Of course I want them to be 'better.' Really, I don't think that someone who's doing the wrong thing with his life ever lives to the fullest. But rather than handing people a set of rules and telling them that these are the rules to follow, I would rather guide them to a closer relationship with God. If their relationship with Him is what it should be, then they really won't need that set of rules. How about you? Is that your primary goal as a deputy, to make people better? Or at least to make them behave?"

"Oh, no," Marilyn replied, biting in to the final scoop

of ice cream. "My job is to protect those who do obey the law. I don't do anything to teach or rehabilitate lawbreakers. I just arrest them and let someone else take them from there." She grinned wickedly. "Someone like you."

"Just what I need," Hunter laughed as he made a face. "Seriously, do you know if any of the other local ministers visit the prison on a regular basis?"

"I've seen Father Donovan over there a few times," Marilyn volunteered as she bit into the crunchy cone. "But I'm sure you'd be welcome. As long as you don't mind the language. The prisoners talk as badly as the deputies."

"And neither one of those groups can hold a candle to sailors," Hunter reminded her. "I'll go over there next week." Marilyn looked at Hunter with genuine admiration. Some of those prisoners were pretty rough types, but, yes, they could probably relate to Hunter where they might not be able to relate to a more conventional minister. Hunter would be good with them.

"So how about you? How did you end up a deputy?" Hunter asked.

"Robert and I trained seven years ago," Marilyn began.

"Robert was your husband?" Hunter asked quietly.

"Yes," Marilyn admitted frankly. "Anyway, I thought I would like the work, so when women's lib came to our small town I applied and was accepted for training. I worked a squad car for a while, then in the office—" Marilyn gulped, thinking of the years that Bobby had been little. "Then after—well, eighteen months ago I asked to be put back in the car. I've done that ever since, except for the occasional assignment like *Wurstfest*."

"Do the men accept you as an equal?" Hunter asked.

Marilyn shrugged and ate the last bite of her cone. "As a good fellow deputy, yes. As their professional equal, no.

But as long as they don't discriminate on my paycheck, what can I say? Attitudes are hard to overcome."

"I'm surprised that you didn't move to San Antonio or Austin after the tragedy and get a job on one of their police forces," Hunter said.

"I thought about it," Marilyn admitted, remembering the desperate longing she had experienced to get away from New Braunfels right after the tragedy. "But this is my home, and frankly most of the small-town folks I come in contact with do respect both the law and the uniform that enforces it. Some of those bastards—uh, suckers—on those city streets can be mean. I'm not sure I'd want to face them on a dark alley at night with just my .38 to protect me."

"You were carrying a .357 the other night," Hunter observed conversationally. "Yours also?"

"Robert's," she replied honestly, surprised that he had noticed the gun. "He left it behind when he moved. I guess he got out of law enforcement."

Hunter did not seem to notice her grim tone. "So tell me about your work. Do you ever get any excitement?"

"Oh, sure," Marilyn replied. "I got involved in a high-speed chase once during my first year on the force that I swear started me on my gray hair. I was riding with a DPS officer—that's Department of Public Safety—as a backup, when out of the blue this Ferrari coming out of San Antonio came tearing up the highway doing at least ninety. My partner chased him at speeds up to 140 until he finally crashed out. The jerk hadn't committed any other crime, just speeding and resisting arrest, but his fine and court costs were nearly a thousand dollars. Not to mention the cost of a new Ferrari."

"Do you get that kind of thing on a regular basis?" Hunter asked.

"No, not really," Marilyn replied. "But there's always

that degree of uncertainty. We just never know what to expect when we get a call. Nineteen times out of twenty it's the wind or an animal that the homeowners hear, but on the twentieth . . ." She shrugged.

"How about the other deputies? Do you like working with them?"

"Most of them are great," Marilyn said warmly. "Even the older men are beginning to come around to women deputies. We do get the occasional weirdo on the reserve force, but then you can't win them all. I had to ride with one once who was a real male chauvinist—he had to be the big shot, handle all the calls, do all the work. So I let him. And then I let him do all the paperwork that went with it! Next time he let me do my share."

"How about Bobby? Did he want to be a deputy, like Mommy and Daddy?" Hunter asked a little too casually.

"Yes," Marilyn replied tersely.

"Tell me about him," Hunter commanded quietly.

Marilyn made a show of looking at her watch. "Oops, Hunter, it's getting late," she said with what she hoped was the properly regretful expression in her voice. "I do have to work this evening. I guess we better go."

Hunter's mouth tightened but he said nothing. He rose abruptly and paid the bill, then escorted Marilyn to her truck. *He's angry because I won't tell him about Bobby,* she thought. *But I just don't want to talk about him. It hurts too much.* She sneaked a look at Hunter out of the corner of her eye. He sat silent, grim-faced, staring out of the window of the truck at the sparse traffic. A small shiver of apprehension slid down her back. Would he let it go, or would he have something to say to her when they got back to the house?

Marilyn parked the big truck in the driveway and hopped out. "Thanks for the ice cream," she said brightly, hoping that Hunter would take the hint and go on home.

She knew that he knew that she was avoiding all talk about her son, but maybe he would understand and not say anything about it. Anyway, she really did have to go on duty soon. "Be seeing you," she added as she bounded up the steps.

Hunter followed her up the steps and waited for a moment while she fumbled in her messy purse for her keys, then impatiently pushed her hand aside and found the keys for her. He inserted the key in the lock and pushed the door open, then gently pushed Marilyn inside and followed her in, shutting the door behind them. "When are you going to stop bottling your grief up inside you?" he demanded imperiously. "When are you going to let it go and get on with your life?"

Marilyn whirled around in shock at the direct attack. "Just because I played for your services like you wanted doesn't give you the right to say that kind of thing to me," she snapped, glaring at him angrily.

"Well, somebody better," Hunter replied, exasperated. "You won't see your old friends, you stay away from the church that you love, you won't even talk about your own son! Somebody needs to talk to you. And everybody else in this town is so afraid of hurting poor Marilyn that they've let you shut yourself off from the only real healing that you're going to find. You're not going to stop hurting by avoiding everything that's going to bring back memories."

"Maybe the people of this town have some compassion," Marilyn replied, stung by his blunt accusations. "Maybe they have a little respect for the kind of sorrow I feel."

"And maybe they're just plain chicken," Hunter taunted. "It would be easier just to leave you alone to brood."

"Then why don't you?" Marilyn shot back. "You come barging in with your good advice and your platitudes, telling me that I should talk about that precious little boy! Damn it, preacher, don't you understand that it hurts to talk about him? I'm trying to forget."

"Listen to me, Marilyn," Hunter said quietly. "I didn't mean to start an argument with you. But I want you to listen and listen good."

"Why should I listen to you?" Marilyn asked peevishly. "You and your—"

"Yes, I'm just full of platitudes," Hunter replied sardonically. "But just remember, lady, that a large chunk of my job involves dealing with just what you've experienced. You're not the first person to suffer the death of a child, and you won't be the last. You do realize that, don't you?" He looked at Marilyn with his piercing black eyes and she nodded wordlessly, feeling like a bug impaled on a pin.

"You're not going to forget your child or what happened to him, so don't even try," Hunter said ruthlessly. Marilyn flinched at the harshness of his words. "Yes, you'll always remember, so shutting your mind to the past isn't going to work. You'll remember him every day for the rest of your life. There's nothing you can do to change that. And I've stood beside my share of caskets and preached when I felt like crying, so I do know what it's like. You don't forget, but you go on."

"I've gone on," Marilyn said defensively. "I kept working, didn't I? I see my friends—my new friends," she amended as Hunter's eyebrow shot up.

"That's all you did," Hunter replied firmly. "You've studiously avoided anything that's going to force you to get over your grief and to get on with living."

"What do you mean, get on with living?" Marilyn asked scornfully. "I'm not dead."

"Inside you are," Hunter replied. "Inside you're almost as dead as Bobby."

Marilyn winced, remembering the many times she had

thought that exact same thing about herself. "Damn you, Hunter Templeton, yes, I'm almost dead inside! What do you expect? I buried the most important person in my life! He was all I cared about!"

"How selfish," Hunter jeered. "You lost the only person whom you cared about, did you? Well, lady, how about the people who care for you? How about your parents, your old friends, the people of the church? Did you bother to notice how glad people were to have you back this morning? Did you ever stop to think how this attitude of yours is hurting the people who love you? Did you ever think of their feelings?"

"Of course I have!" Marilyn yelled at him. "Do you think I like feeling like a Popsicle inside? Do you think that this empty limbo is fun? Do you honestly think I haven't seen the hurt and worry in their faces? Do you really think I like hurting them?"

"Then why don't you do something about it?" Hunter asked quietly.

"What?" Marilyn asked flatly. "It's not that I don't want to come back to life, Hunter. It's that I just can't. Do you hear me? I just can't."

"Oh, yes, you can," Hunter said softly, moving with the quiet stealth of a cat. Before Marilyn even realized what he had in mind, he had taken her into his arms and was pulling her close to him. "Oh, yes, lady, you most certainly can come back to life."

My God, he can't do this to me, Marilyn thought as his mouth came down on hers, pushing her lips open and plundering the depths of her sweetness. His tongue snaked around the insides of her lips, stunning Marilyn with its sensual, erotic touch on the sensitive flesh that it encountered. Marilyn tried to pull away, but Hunter's arms held her firmly, tightly, to the hard length of his body. Slowly his lips and his tongue tormented her, gradually turning her outrage into another emotion, an emotion that frightened Marilyn much more than Hunter himself did. Desperately she tried to wrench her mouth away, but Hunter brought up one of his strong hands and held her head steady while he continued the sensual assault on her tender mouth. Marilyn's senses were whirling. Emotions that she thought she had buried when Robert walked out had come screaming back to life, startling her with their urgent demands. She had to get out of this embrace before she gave in to it. "Hunter, no," she murmured against his insistent lips.

"Marilyn, yes," Hunter whispered as he tightened his hold on her, yet at the same time he slackened the suffocating pressure on her mouth to the point where his was only teasing hers erotically, tormenting her into response. His direct assault Marilyn could resist; these tempting caresses she could not.

Slowly, without even being aware of her surrender, Marilyn moved ever so imperceptibly toward Hunter and sought his warm firm lips with her own. Hunter returned her welcome, and they shared a long mutual kiss that could have gone on forever. Hunter released her head and ran his hands down her arms and settled them into her slender waist, fanning his fingers on her hips. Marilyn slid her arms up around his neck, finding the coarse blond hair at his nape and locking her fingers into it. Her breasts were crushed against Hunter's strong chest, and the pressure from his hard, muscular body made them tingle with anticipation. More, more! her body cried, wanting to further explore this passionate caress.

Slowly Hunter released Marilyn's mouth and eased her body away from his. Reluctant to leave his embrace, she looked up at him beseechingly and stared at him in confusion, then as she realized what had just happened she colored in mortification. She had wanted Hunter to go on kissing her, holding her, touching her. Aghast, she pulled away from his arms and walked across the floor with unsteady legs.

"Marilyn, look at me," Hunter said softly. "Marilyn!" he said when she did not turn around.

Slowly Marilyn turned around and looked at him with wide, round eyes. Hunter was breathing as hard as she was, and his eyes were covered with the fine glaze of passion. Gratified that he, too, had been affected by the embrace, she stared at him questioningly.

"You can come back to life," he said simply. "For a few moments there in my arms, you did." Without giving Marilyn a chance to reply, Hunter turned on his heel and left the house, slamming the door behind him.

"Damn you, Hunter Templeton," Marilyn whispered at his retreating back. "Damn you to hell!"

Marilyn knotted her uniform tie and looked at herself critically. Her lips were a little swollen, but they were not bruised, for despite his passion and his determination to kiss her fully, Hunter had been gentle. But it was her eyes that gave her away. The opaque mask of grief had been stripped away, replaced by the bemused passion that Hunter had bewildered her with this afternoon. How could she have responded to him like that? A man who was trying to run her life for her, a man who she wished would just leave her alone! Oh, but she had not wanted to respond to him. She had wanted to remain aloof, but she simply could not help but come alive in his arms. Why couldn't he have picked another way to make his point? *Damn him, even if he is a preacher!* Marilyn thought as she strapped on her Sam Brown with trembling fingers.

But Hunter had proved a point. She was not dead inside and had come back to life with a vengeance! At least the sexual side of her nature had. *Maybe that's all it is,* Marilyn said to herself as she grabbed her jacket and headed out the front door. *Maybe it's just sex.*

"Oh, Marilyn, do you have a minute?" Doris Bettencourt trilled as Marilyn locked the front door behind her. *Oh, no,* Marilyn thought as she glanced at her watch. Doris was a dear, but she was such a busybody! No telling what gossip she was just dying to pour into Marilyn's ear. Oh, well, she had a few minutes. And it might be good for a laugh. She could sure use one about now.

"Oh, Marilyn, it was so good to see you and hear you play in church this morning." Doris sighed as she patted Marilyn's arm with a small plump hand. "It was so good not to have to listen to Mrs. Weissmann's mistakes."

"Thank you," Marilyn said. *At least, I think that was a compliment. Okay, Doris, come on with the gossip,* she thought.

"And doesn't Reverend Templeton preach a fine message?" Doris continued. "And him being so young and all."

"He's not all that young," Marilyn replied. "He's older than I am."

"Oh, but when you're my age, he's young," Doris replied, touching her silver hair teasingly. *So we're going to gossip about the minister,* Marilyn thought. "And such a fine-looking young preacher! Why, he's enough to put the hearts of his single ladies to beating right fast, isn't he?"

"I—I really wouldn't know," Marilyn stammered, hoping that her red cheeks wouldn't give her away.

"Why, I could have sworn I saw him on your doorstep earlier this afternoon," Doris replied, as subtle as a Sherman tank. "I thought he might have come to see you."

"He did come over this afternoon," Marilyn replied steadily, forcing herself to remain calm. *So we're going to gossip about Marilyn and the minister,* she amended to herself. "We went for ice cream," she added reluctantly.

If everybody in New Braunfels was going to know about it, they might as well get their facts straight.

"Oh, how nice!" Doris replied, clapping her hands together. "And he's such a sexy man! I do love a good romance! Oh, Marilyn, I'm so excited!"

"Doris, there's no romance!" Marilyn protested. "Only ice cream. Honestly." Oh, no, where had Doris gotten the idea that she thought of Hunter in a romantic way?

"That's all right, Marilyn, I can keep a secret!" Doris crooned as she patted Marilyn's arm sympathetically. *Sure you can,* Marilyn thought as she watched Doris walk back to her own front porch across the street. *You'll be on the telephone before I get the truck started.* Doris's front windows were open and the late afternoon sunlight streamed in, filling the small living room with a soft pink glow. Sure enough, Doris headed straight for the telephone stand and picked up the receiver.

The window! Marilyn whirled around and gasped in dismay. Her own drapes were open and her living room was as well-illuminated as Doris's had been. And she and Hunter had been right in front of the window. Doris had seen everything! Disgruntled, Marilyn climbed into the truck and looked at her face in the rearview mirror. Yes, she still looked thoroughly kissed. Doris had noticed that, too, of course. And she was on the telephone right now, spreading the good news. *Hooray,* Marilyn thought as she slammed the truck into gear and backed out of the driveway. *Hunter Templeton, I could kill you for this!*

Hunter whistled as he opened a can of chili and dumped it into a saucepan. *Well, you really woke her up, fella. Yes, you definitely breathed some life back into the lady!* He got out a loaf of bread and broke off a third of a head of lettuce, which he drenched with bottled dressing and put on the table. But, Hunter had to admit to himself, she had shaken him up too.

Hunter dished up the chili and sat down. Yes, Marilyn had shaken him to the core, more deeply than he had thought possible. His own tender feelings, which he had ruthlessly buried with the defection of his fiancée so long ago, had come rushing back with such sensual strength that it had been all he could do to let Marilyn go. Hunter winced a little as the spicy chili stung his bruised lips. She had returned his embrace so passionately. Robert Davis had been a fool to leave her, that was for sure.

So what about Marilyn? Hunter wondered as he ate his simple supper. *I showed her that she can respond physically, and that's a start, but what about the rest of her? What about the inside? What about that part of her that won't face the hurt?* Hunter sipped his iced tea and stared into space. *I'm glad she responded physically to me,* he thought, *even if I will be taking cold showers for a week. But that's only her surface emotion. The interior of her is still frozen, and she'll never be right as long as it is. Now, how can I get through to that frozen spirit inside of her?*

Marilyn parked the squad car and killed the engine. "Thank God that shift's over," she said wearily as she climbed out of the car and rubbed her back a little.

Tess got out on the other side and pulled the door shut behind her. "I was tempted to strangle that little old lady out at Canyon Lake," she said frankly as they walked together into the sheriff's office. The stubborn little woman had insisted that there was a prowler on her lot, and Tess and Marilyn had spent the better part of an hour in a cold rain looking for a prowler who simply didn't exist. As a result, they were late returning to the office, and the others on their shift had long ago turned in their keys and headed for home.

Marilyn handed her keys to the deputy manning the desk and dug down in her pocket for her own keys. It took a bit of fumbling, but she finally fished them out, wishing momentarily that Hunter had been there to find them for her. Tess found her own keys, then sighed and turned to Marilyn. "You know, I'm tired but not really sleepy. Want to go out for a cup of coffee?"

"At three in the morning? A nice girl like me?" Marilyn teased. "I'll follow you to the truck stop, and I'll eat and watch you drink your coffee."

"Fair enough," Tess said.

A few minutes later they were sitting across from each other in the truck stop on I-35, about the only place that was open at this hour. The bored waitress took their order, and the few tired truckers that were in the place ignored them completely. Marilyn admitted to herself that they might have been approached if they had not been in uniform.

"So what's this I hear about you smoochin' on the new preacher?" Tess asked Marilyn, a wicked grin on her face.

Marilyn's head shot up, her face flaming. "My God, is it all over town?" she groaned.

"Just about," Tess replied cheerfully, laughing at Marilyn's embarrassment. "I've heard it from three different people this week, and it was the topic this afternoon in the teachers' lounge." Tess sighed in mock sorrow.

"Oh, no," Marilyn cried. "Does everybody know? I'm going to kill that man, I really am!"

"So why do you want to kill him if you were kissing on him like that?" Tess asked innocently, loving every moment of Marilyn's misery. The waitress brought Tess's coffee and a piece of apple pie for Marilyn.

Marilyn tasted her pie and made a face. "Too sweet," she said. "He wasn't really kissing me, Tess," she explained as she nibbled on a bite of the pie.

"That isn't what Doris Bettencourt said." Tess giggled, sipping her coffee. "She said it was better than those torrid scenes on the afternoon soaps," she snickered.

"Hunter was not kissing me. He was proving a point," Marilyn said with great dignity.

The laughter faded from Tess's face. "And what point could that possibly have been?" she asked curiously.

"I told him that I couldn't come back to life, really live, since Bobby's death. He said that I could, and kissed me to prove it."

"Well, what was the verdict?" Tess asked. "Can you?"

"Can I what? Come back to life?" Marilyn stopped and blushed furiously. "I don't know, but apparently Hunter thinks so," she said as she sipped her glass of water.

"Well, good for Hunter!" Tess said enthusiastically. "It's about time something shook you up!"

"*Tess!*" Marilyn cried, spilling water on the table. She wiped it up and eyed her friend incredulously.

"I mean it, Marilyn," Tess said seriously. "You've been brooding too long. It's about time somebody reached into your little shell and pulled you out."

"I am not in a shell," Marilyn replied, "and I'm not brooding. I work, I go out, I have friends . . ."

"Oh, I know you have friends on the force, and you go through the motions, but you're a long way from being all right." Tess looked at Marilyn thoughtfully. "Anybody who would continue to cut herself off from the circle of friends like you had up at that church can't be over the grief."

"Not you too, Tess," Marilyn replied dryly. "You sound like Hunter."

"So? The man has a point, Marilyn," Tess said gently. "I don't know, maybe I've been wrong in not saying something to you sooner. I've been worried about you for months, but I didn't want to say anything that would hurt you or push you away. But Marilyn, you can't go on the way you have been and expect to come to grips with the tragedy. By cutting off your old friends and your church, you're leaving an unhealed wound, a large one, that's going to fester sooner or later, if it hasn't already."

"But it hurts . . ." Marilyn began.

"Of course it hurts," Tess replied gently as she sipped her coffee. "It hurts my kids when I scrub the dirt out of a cut, doesn't it? But if I don't, the wound doesn't heal properly. It's the same with you. You need to go back to church, see your old friends again, and face the pain squarely. You played for church last week, didn't you?" Marilyn nodded. "So how was it?" Tess asked. "Did it hurt?"

"Yes," Marilyn replied.

"Is it going to hurt so much next week?" Tess asked shrewdly.

"No—no, I don't think it will," Marilyn admitted.

"You see?" Tess pressed on. "And after a few weeks, maybe it won't hurt at all. You'll have recovered from at least that part of your grief. Now, with your old friends it would be the same way."

"It would be worse," Marilyn said quickly. "Tess, they have little children! Those kids used to play with Bobby! Every time I'd look at those little ones, I'd remember Bobby, and I can't take that!" Her hands started to shake and her chin trembled.

"Hey, don't get upset," Tess said as she reached out and put her hand on Marilyn's trembling arm. "I don't know, maybe you're not ready for that yet. But soon you will be, and you'll have to see those people again and face the hurt, because that will be the only way you will ever be whole again. Marilyn, right now you're only half alive. Do you want to stay that way?"

"That's what Hunter said," Marilyn said glumly, pushing the too-sweet pie away in disgust.

"He's right," Tess replied forcefully. "But I don't buy the bit about him kissing you just to prove a point. He could have made his point in any number of ways. A man like Hunter doesn't kiss a woman like he kissed you unless he means it."

"How do you know how he kissed me?" Marilyn demanded, blushing furiously.

"Doris had just cleaned her glasses," Tess replied sardonically. "You know, Marilyn, a romance with Hunter might be just the thing for you."

"Tess, you can't mean that!" Marilyn gasped. "It wouldn't be proper!"

"You've been divorced for over a year," Tess corrected her gently. "You're free to see Hunter if you want to."

"But he's a preacher!" Marilyn continued, grasping for excuses.

"So? That's not a problem in your church, is it?" Tess asked. "Aren't most of your ministers married?"

"Tess, I am *not* going to have a romance with Hunter or any other man," Marilyn replied firmly.

"Well, I bet you're wrong about that," Tess said smugly, draining her coffee cup. "That preacher has his eye on you." She grinned wickedly. "And if that handsome hunk can have you blushing instead of grieving, he has my permission to kiss you at twelve noon on Main Street if he wants to."

"Thanks a million," Marilyn said dryly, and changed the subject, but as she drove home in the still of the early morning, she pondered Tess's attitude. She had not realized that Tess felt that strongly about her continued grieving or her absence from the church, and she was frankly surprised that Tess had cheered Hunter on. Marilyn frowned as she parked the truck in the driveway. Tess was one of the few people whose opinion she really trusted, so if Tess thought she wasn't facing the hurt, then maybe she wasn't. But a romance with Hunter? *Tess, you have to be kidding,* Marilyn thought even as her heartbeat quickened momentarily.

Marilyn dragged herself into the house and shut the front door behind her, tiredly flopping down on the couch and easing off one boot after the other. So maybe Tess was right. Maybe she was only half alive. So what could she do about it? A crimson blush crept up her cheeks as she remembered Hunter's passionate kiss the other afternoon. He had shown her exactly what to do!

CHAPTER FOUR

Marilyn sat in the patrol car along the edge of the road and watched the cattle grazing on the other side of the fence, the cold November wind ruffling the short hair on their broad sides. She sighed with boredom and pushed her wire-rimmed sunglasses back up her nose. It had been one of the slowest days in her years on the force, and Marilyn longed for the familiar crackle of the radio, so that she could drive somewhere and do something. She was bored enough to scream. She had answered exactly two calls since eight this morning, and she had dealt with both in a matter of minutes and had spent the remainder of the day sitting along the edge of the road, ostensibly watching for speeders.

Boyd had hinted to all the deputies that the coffers were low and that he wanted more tickets issued between Thanksgiving and Christmas. Thanksgiving had been yesterday, so that left the deputies only about five weeks to reform the driving habits of Comal County to Boyd's satisfaction.

Grimacing a little at the unfair practice, Marilyn nevertheless complied with it because Boyd was the boss, and if Boyd wanted her to issue more tickets, then she would. But today she didn't even seem able to do that, since every car and truck on the road since early this morning had been traveling at a reasonable rate of speed. "I guess everyone in New Braunfels knows we're out today," Marilyn griped out loud in the empty car.

"Spoke too soon!" she yelped a minute later when an old green Mustang whizzed by doing at least seventy. "Whoever you are, you just sped by the wrong lady," she whooped as she pulled out onto the road quickly and put on her lights. At the rate at which the Mustang was traveling, it took her a little time to catch up with it, and Marilyn wondered as she gained on the car just who would drive a funny-looking old vehicle like that. She bet that it was at least fifteen years old and hadn't had a fresh paint job in all its years. As she got closer, she noticed that the left fender had a small dent in it, but she gathered as the little car finally spotted her and pulled over that there was nothing wrong with it under the hood.

Marilyn grabbed up her ticket book and hopped out of the squad car, preparing to face a belligerent teenager who was in turn going to have to face an exasperated father later tonight. But she gasped in shock when Hunter Templeton rolled down the window and handed her his driver's license, grinning sheepishly.

She had not spoken directly to Hunter since he had kissed her so passionately in her living room three weeks before, and a crimson stain crept up her face as she remembered her abandoned response to him. Although she had played for two more services since then, she had ducked out the door without speaking to him, not knowing or caring if her obvious reluctance to speak to him was quelling the gossip about them or only feeding it. More than once in the last three weeks she had caught herself reliving that torrid embrace, and she wondered if Hunter had found her as hard to dismiss as she had him.

She took the driver's license from him and read it, surprised to find out that Hunter was thirty-nine, since he hadn't seemed that old to her. "Aren't you a little old to be burning up the road like that?" she asked, a smile playing around the corner of her mouth.

Hunter blushed furiously, his face burning brightly under his fair head of hair. "So now you know my favorite vice," he mumbled as Marilyn laughed out loud at his discomfort.

"You're a public menace!" she said with mock fierceness, then she laughed out loud at his obvious discomfort. For once she had the upper hand, and she was enjoying it. "Tell me, is there one of them-there fancy racing engines under this mild-mannered little old hood?"

"I wasn't going that fast," Hunter protested.

"Reverend Templeton, my dear Reverend Templeton, you were going seventy if you were going a mile. I hate to remind you, but with the Lord's blessing the law of the land was changed to fifty-five some years ago."

"I know," Hunter grumbled, then his face split and they laughed together. "But look at it this way, Marilyn," he added with a twinkle in his eye, "at least you know that you'll never have to haul me in for DWI."

"That's true," she acknowledged as she mentally calculated the fine for going fifteen miles over the speed limit and winced when she arrived at the figure. "But this is going to be bad enough," she muttered under her breath.

"That bad, huh?" Hunter asked, his face falling.

I bet I just ruined his day, Marilyn thought as she took in the old car and Hunter's ironed but far from new shirt. Although she had seen the church budget and knew that Hunter wasn't destitute, she also knew that he probably had to be pretty careful with his money, and the fine would seriously dent his weekly budget. She bit her lip and started to write the ticket, then remembered the way that Hunter had carried that drunk to the trailer for her and Tess at *Wurstfest. Sorry, Boyd,* she thought as she lifted her pen and flipped to the back of the book. The sheriff's department owes him one. She quickly wrote out a warning and handed it to Hunter.

He read the ticket and looked at her, the relief obvious

on his face. "Thanks, Marilyn," he said softly. "It would have been hard going paying that ticket."

Marilyn nodded. "I knew that," she said softly. Then she firmed her mouth and gave him her best deputy scowl. "But I don't want you thinking that it's all right to speed on these roads, and I'll tell you why. On the Interstates it's all right if you can get away with it because you always have the left lane to go into. But out here on these two-lane farm-to-markets, especially the ones that twist around in these hills like this one does, you could come up on a slower moving vehicle and rear-end them before you know what you're doing, especially if there's someone coming in the opposite direction and you can't go into that lane. Just last year that happened a few miles from here and it was nasty."

Hunter looked suitably chastened. "Sorry, I didn't realize," he said softly.

"Please, remember it," Marilyn said, her voice softening. "You would be in one of the cars, you know."

Hunter nodded his head, then looked up and grinned. "And if I get stopped on the Interstate, can I tell the highway patrolman that you said it was all right?"

Marilyn swiped at his nose with the ticket book. "Why don't you try your jokes in the pulpit?" she asked as she laughed in spite of herself.

"Because I want to stay at that church," Hunter replied honestly. "Look, I appreciate you not giving me that ticket. Are you free this weekend? Maybe we could drive down to San Antonio for dinner."

"Oh, I don't know, Hunter," Marilyn started to stammer, shaking her head. The memory of his kiss flew to the forefront of her mind, and now she was blushing to the roots of her hair. "I'm not—I don't . . ."

"Well, how about if I don't kiss you unless you want me

to?" Hunter asked with laughter in his eyes as Marilyn's blush deepened.

"It could be construed as a bribe," Marilyn replied lamely. "I didn't give you the ticket, and you take me out to dinner."

"Nonsense," Hunter replied firmly. "I didn't ask you out until after you had written the warning. Are you free tomorrow night? Yes or no. And don't lie to your minister."

"Yes, I'm free," Marilyn said impatiently. "Although you do realize that it's quite all right to fib to a common lawbreaker, don't you?"

"I just became the preacher again," Hunter said smoothly. "I'll pick you up at seven, and wear something pretty. I'll take you someplace nice. 'Bye, hon," he called as he rolled up the window and drove away, leaving Marilyn standing by the side of the road feeling like she had been run over by a steamroller.

Now, why didn't I just tell him no? Marilyn wondered as she climbed back into the squad car and put it in gear. *Damn it, he's doing it again, butting in and getting me to do things his way.* But, Marilyn had to admit, as she picked up the crackling radio and answered a call, that she was looking forward to the evening with him.

Marilyn bent over the tomatoes and poked around gently, hoping to find a decent tomato for her salad tonight. She squeezed one a little and grimaced as she felt the baseball-hard vegetable in her palm. *Now, how am I supposed to eat that?* she groused to herself as she put the tomato aside and felt another one. It wasn't much better, but it gave a little to her touch, so Marilyn dropped it into her sack and touched another one. It too was hard as a rock. "This is hopeless," she muttered as she put the tomato back on the pile.

"Are they that bad?" a familiar voice asked at her elbow.

Marilyn whirled around at the woman's voice. "Suzanne! How are you?" Marilyn asked as she peeked around the woman. Spotting no one behind her, Marilyn sighed inwardly in relief.

"Oh, Marilyn, I didn't even recognize you in that uniform," Suzanne laughed as she reached out and hugged Marilyn. "I'm okay. And how about you? We never see you at church anymore."

"Then you haven't been recently," Marilyn teased, wagging her finger in Suzanne's face. "I've been playing for the last three weeks."

Suzanne blushed. "Well, we haven't been in the last month or so—you're right. We've had some sickness in the family." Marilyn noticed that Suzanne looked tired.

"I'm sorry to hear that," Marilyn said honestly. "That flu bug?"

"Well, sort of," Suzanne said hesitantly. At that moment a small blond boy came out from behind the water fountain and ran up to Suzanne, hugging her around the legs. "Watch out, Ryan, you're going to knock me over," his mother cautioned him.

Marilyn stared, mesmerized, at little Ryan Bohannon, the little boy who had been Bobby's best friend. She had thought that Suzanne was in the store alone and that she would not have to see the child and expose herself to the tearing memories of the two children together. Ryan and Bobby crawling across the floor, taking their first steps within days of each other, fighting over a prized toy, squirting water at each other in Bobby's plastic wading pool. She looked down at the small boy and felt a moment of bitterness that Ryan was still alive and that Bobby was gone. Firmly chiding herself for even feeling such a thing toward an innocent child, she reached down and ruffled

Ryan's hair. "How are you, Ryan?" she asked in a broken voice.

Ryan looked up at her in puzzlement for a moment, then his face cleared. "You're Bobby's mommy," he said.

"Yes, honey, I'm Bobby's mommy," she said with a thick throat.

She looked up at Suzanne and saw that Suzanne had tears in her eyes. "He still remembers Bobby," Suzanne said softly.

"Yeah, my mommy said that Bobby's in heaven with Jesus," Ryan volunteered. "He can see Jesus when he talks to him."

Marilyn smiled in spite of the tears in her eyes. "That's right, hon, he sure can." She took a deep breath. "So how about you, Ryan? How old are you now?"

"I'll be five next month," he said proudly, then rushed into speech. "If you're Bobby's mommy, why are you wearing that policeman's suit?"

Marilyn looked at Suzanne and laughed. "I guess he never saw me in uniform, did he? Well, Ryan," she said, kneeling down so that he could see her better, "I'm a sheriff's deputy."

While she let Ryan look at her uniform, she looked carefully at him and was surprised to note that the little boy was virtually no taller than he had been the last time he and Bobby had played, and that he was thin—too thin. He had deep, dark circles under the little blue eyes that were darting over her uniform with the innocent curiosity of a child. *I guess the flu really got to the little fellow,* she thought, remembering the way sturdy little Bobby threw off almost everything he ever caught. But a bout of flu wouldn't be responsible for Ryan's not growing, she mused with puzzlement.

Ryan reached over and touched her gun gingerly. "Is that your gun?" he asked curiously.

"Yes, that's my gun," Marilyn replied patiently.

"Do you kill people with it?" he asked.

"Ryan!" Suzanne gasped as Marilyn started laughing helplessly. "Of course she doesn't kill people with it!"

Marilyn fought to get her laughter under control, then looked up at the embarrassment on Suzanne's face and started laughing again.

"No, Ryan, I don't kill people with it. I try to help them." She reached out and gave the child a quick hug, and realized with a shock that the little boy was almost emaciated under his cotton shirt. She stood up and looked at Suzanne, noting that Suzanne had lost weight, too, and was looking not only tired, but pinched and strained around the mouth. She opened her mouth to say something, then stopped herself. What could she say? You just didn't come out and ask a mother why she and her child both looked like hell. Instead she smiled at them both. "Well, since I'm playing again, at least for a few more Sundays, maybe I'll see you in church soon," she said as she looked down at Ryan again, the pain of her own sorrow muted by her concern for the child who stood in front of her.

"I hope so," Suzanne said quietly as she took Ryan's hand. "It was good to see you, Marilyn," she added as they wandered toward the dairy section.

Marilyn watched them go, hand in hand, chattering happily as they rounded the corner. *Bobby and I would have been like that,* she thought sadly as she wheeled her basket around and headed for checkout. Even if her child was sick, Suzanne Bohannon was lucky.

Marilyn deftly ringed her eyes with brown eyeliner and smudged it carefully, then she smoothed on a shimmering gray shadow and blended it to her brow. *Very nice,* she thought, quickly adding mascara and a little bit of cover-stick to the faint circles under her eyes that would not seem to go away, no matter how much sleep she had. And she had been sleeping better these days, she mused as she smoothed on a light coat of foundation and a glossy pink lipstick. Much better. Instead of brooding about Bobby for hours on end, she found to her astonishment that she was drifting off to sleep after only a few minutes, waking in the morning feeling refreshed instead of miserable. Not understanding why, Marilyn was nevertheless grateful for this change, and hummed under her breath as she rifled through her closet for a dress that met Hunter's specifications. Pretty, he wanted. How about this? She took out the dress that she had made the year she went to a costume party as a call girl and held it up to herself. She laughed out loud as she pictured Hunter's reaction if she were to appear in that provocative outfit. No, she wouldn't do that to him.

Finally settling on a simply cut rose dress that had been in her wardrobe for several years, she pulled it over her head as the doorbell rang. She zipped it up as quickly as she could and ran in her stocking feet to the front door, opening it wide and smiling warmly at Hunter as he stepped inside. Without the heels of either her shoes or her boots, Marilyn was conscious for the first time of how Hunter towered over her. He was dressed in an open-necked cream shirt and matching slacks with a tan sport coat. Marilyn swallowed as a wave of desire flooded through her, and she fought the urge to reach out and touch this virile man. Instead, she motioned for him to sit down.

"Can I get you a drink?" she asked out of habit, then berated herself for what she had said. "I mean, uh, I don't, but Robert used to offer it to his friends and . . ." She broke off her stammering when she realized that Hunter was openly laughing at her.

"Marilyn, you're priceless," he laughed. "Tell me, do you have orange juice in this den of iniquity?"

"As a matter of fact, I do," Marilyn said as she escaped to the kitchen, opening the refrigerator with trembling fingers. *Marilyn, you must be rattled. Offering the preacher a drink!* She poured them both orange juice and returned to the living room.

They made small talk while they drank their juice, then Marilyn found her shoes and her purse and picked up a lacy but substantial shawl and wrapped it around her.

"Shall we go?" Hunter asked as she returned to the room.

Marilyn nodded, her throat suddenly dry. This was her first real date, not counting the afternoon in the ice cream parlor, since her divorce, and she discovered to her astonishment that she was nervous. She hadn't been on a date in years. What on earth would they talk about all evening? Hunter opened the car door for her and she climbed in, noticing with amusement that the little old Mustang had been freshly washed and the junk cleaned out of it.

Hunter climbed in on the driver's side and switched on the ignition, then noticed the expression on Marilyn's face and looked at her worriedly. "Are you all right?" he asked with concern.

Marilyn smiled at him sheepishly. "I'm nervous," she admitted. "I haven't been on a date in years, and I don't know what to do anymore."

Hunter tried to look at her with reassurance, but his amusement got the better of him and he chuckled softly. "Well, I don't think it's changed much in the last few years. You do the same things that went on back when you were dating."

"Grope and dodge?" Marilyn asked dryly, then they both laughed, the tension in Marilyn fading.

"Well, you never know," Hunter said, leering at her

wickedly and leaning toward her. "If I'm going to preach on the evils of the flesh, maybe I better find out a little bit about them!"

"And you want little angelic me to teach you?" Marilyn teased, batting her eyes at him. "I'm afraid you picked the wrong teacher!"

"Aw, shucks," Hunter said, his face falling in mock disappointment. "And here I was going to have *the* best sermon." They were both still laughing as Hunter pulled out of her driveway and headed for San Antonio.

Marilyn's nervousness gone, she chattered with Hunter all the way into the big city that was only a few miles away from New Braunfels but that was so different from it. Expecting to eat at one of the restaurants that lined the north side of the city, Marilyn was surprised when Hunter drove deep into the heart of the city and through the narrow streets of downtown. Although it was only the Saturday after Thanksgiving, Christmas decorations brightened the windows of the department stores and street corners. Hunter drove into the entrance of the old Hemisfair complex and pulled into the Tower of the Americas parking lot. "Heights don't bother you, do they?" he asked casually.

Marilyn craned her neck and looked up at the Hemisfair Tower. "You want to eat up there?" she asked in surprise. "That will cost more than the ticket would have!"

Hunter shrugged eloquently. "But it will be a lot more fun," he said softly.

"Then I'd love it," Marilyn said firmly.

They rode in the outside elevator, Marilyn holding tightly to Hunter's hand as they swooped upward, six hundred feet above the city. His hand felt hard and callused, and Marilyn wondered what a minister would do to get calluses like that. The touch of his palm in hers was warm and tender, yet sensual in a way, and Marilyn enjoyed the chaste contact with him. She was vaguely disappointed when Hunter let go of her hand, but immediately he placed his hand on the small of her back and directed her toward the headwaiter. "Templeton for two," he said softly.

The waiter escorted them toward the slowly revolving dining room. "Be careful, ma'am," he said as Marilyn stepped across onto the revolving platform that held the tables. The waiter took them to a window table and seated them across from each other, then lit the little oil lamp on their table, removed the extra knives and forks, and handed them both a menu and left them.

"Alone at last!" Hunter teased as Marilyn gazed out at the lights of the city, even brighter than usual from the Christmas lights that adorned the downtown area. Hunter flicked open his menu, but soon he, too, was gazing out the window as their table slowly traveled around the city. "Pretty, isn't it?" he asked softly.

"Um-hm," Marilyn murmured. She drew herself away from the beautiful view long enough to select a delicious-sounding chicken dish from the menu, and Hunter looked swiftly at his menu, then set it aside. They returned their gaze to the bright, colorful panorama that unfolded below them, saying little but comfortably enjoying the view.

The waiter brought them water and took their orders. Hunter leaned back in his chair and folded his arms across his chest. "So how have you been?" he asked softly. "Really?"

Marilyn did not pretend to misunderstand. "Better. Much better," she said with a faint smile on her face. "At least I can sleep at night again."

"And playing for church?" Hunter asked.

"Well, it still hurts, and sometimes I still get flashes of

the way the flowers looked the day Bobby was buried. But on the whole I guess it's going to be all right."

"So do you think you'll be willing to continue on a permanent basis?" Hunter asked.

"Ah-ha! That's what dinner was all about!" Marilyn teased as she waved her finger in Hunter's face, laughing as he started to shake his head vigorously. "I'm just giving you a hard time, Hunter," she assured him. "But seriously, I've pulled all manner of strings to make it four Sundays in a row. Boyd made it clear that he was doing me a very big favor and that I better not expect it forever. But when I'm not at work, I'll play. Fair enough?"

"Fair enough," Hunter said as he reached across the table and shook her hand. He sat for a moment, a hesitant expression on his face. "One more request," he said softly.

"Fire away," Marilyn said.

"Would you be able to get there tomorrow in time to play for one of the Sunday school classes? Susan Thomas usually plays for them, but she's out of town."

"Why not?" Marilyn said, shrugging her shoulders. Hunter started to say something but at that moment their salads arrived and their attention was diverted.

Dinner was delightful. Marilyn's Hawaiian chicken served on a bed of rice was delicious, and Hunter seemed equally pleased with his steak and shrimp. They laughed and talked about many things, Marilyn telling him about the funny things that she and her older sister had done to their mother and dad when they were kids, and all the things she and her gang had done in high school, causing Hunter to wonder aloud if all the present deputies had spent that much time on the wrong side of the law.

Hunter in turn entertained her with stories of his days in the navy, reducing her to helpless laughter over some of the hijinks that he and the other sailors managed to get into during their shore leaves in Vietnam. He told her about some of the amusing incidents that had gone on in the seminary, and together they compared notes of all the hilarious things they had seen go wrong during church services. Hunter told with great relish of the time that he mistakenly called for the benediction instead of the invocation and how half of the congregation had gotten up to leave when the prayer was over. Marilyn told him about the time that the binding on her hymnal was too stiff and her music would not lay flat. In desperation she had picked up the book and cracked it, then had watched in dismay as her music, along with half of the rest of the book, had fallen out and come sliding down the keys, Marilyn desperately trying to play and grab her music at the same time. As though by mutual consent, she and Hunter did not mention Bobby or anything about the time when he was alive.

"Dinner was delicious," Marilyn said with a warm smile as the waiter left with the check and Hunter's money. "I enjoyed it thoroughly."

"So did I," Hunter said softly, smiling at Marilyn with such sensual appeal that it was all she could do to stay on her own side of the table. Mesmerized, she gazed at him, circling her lips lightly with her tongue in a gesture that was unconsciously provocative.

They stood up and he extended his hand, leading her wordlessly to the elevator marked Observation Deck. They took the short ride up to the highest level of the Tower, and together they wandered past the souvenir booth and through the glass doors to the outside deck. Marilyn shivered as the cool wind blew into her face, ruffling her hair and blowing her skirt out behind her. At this late hour the observation deck was almost deserted, populated only by a couple of Air Force recruits and Marilyn and Hunter.

"Cold?" Hunter asked as he slid his arm around Marilyn's shoulders.

She nodded and cuddled into his comforting warmth, the heat from his body radiating through his jacket and shirt. Slowly they strolled around the deck, Marilyn pointing out a few San Antonio landmarks to Hunter, who was not as familiar with the city as she was. Hunter's body was hard and exciting against her own, and in spite of her natural reserve Marilyn felt herself melting into him.

Hunter stopped on the far side of the deck, away from the doors, and turned her around gently to face him. The warm, sensual look on his face sent shivers through Marilyn's body. "I'm going to kiss you again," Hunter said softly. "Because you want me to. And it isn't going to be like the last time."

Marilyn swayed toward him, a soft smile on her lips. "Isn't this nice," she said softly. "Doris isn't watching us tonight."

Hunter's lips curled into a smile, then he bent his head and touched her mouth with his own. Marilyn's response was instantaneous. She arched her body and met his lips fervently, giving in to the unconscious desire she had felt all evening to kiss and caress Hunter Templeton. Slowly her arms twined around his neck, pulling him nearer, and she thrust her body closer to his. For a moment or two Hunter let her take the initiative and set the pace, his arms holding her only lightly, then he gathered her to him with all the tenderness and passion that he possessed, hooking his arm around her waist and anchoring her firmly, and with his other arm making delicate forays up and down her spine. Lightly, delicately, his tongue probed the softness of her lips, and Marilyn opened herself to him.

Marilyn let her arms drift down Hunter's solid chest, reveling in the feel of the hard muscles under her fingers, their sinewy texture tense with longing. Slowly he eased his mouth from hers, to move his lips delicately across her face, painting it with tender little kisses until he had reached her ear, where his tongue traced the smooth shell, the moisture from his mouth cool in the night wind.

Marilyn reached up and kissed his jaw softly, tickling his neck with tender caresses. Hunter let one hand slide around her and touch one breast softly, fingering it gently as it became a hard knot beneath the fabric of her silky dress. They touched gently for a few moments, then Hunter drew her to him and kissed her again, pouring all the tenderness and passion that he could into the embrace. Marilyn, so long starved for love, returned his tenderness, giving in to all the dammed-up emotion that she had denied for so long. The cold wind buffeted them unmercifully, but they did not care, wrapped in each other's arms as they were. They clung for long moments, unmindful of time, neither wanting to end the embrace.

Finally Hunter drew back, his eyes glazed. "I better take you home," he whispered, his voice strangely husky.

Marilyn nodded, too moved to speak. They went down the elevator and walked to the car in silence. Neither had much to say on the way back to New Braunfels, but the atmosphere was not strained. Instead, they seemed content to hold hands and murmur an occasional comment as the miles sped past.

As they pulled into Marilyn's driveway, Hunter killed the engine and turned to Marilyn. "Thank you for coming out with me," he said softly.

"Thank you," Marilyn said, her face still bemused. "I had a wonderful time."

"I'm glad," Hunter said as he reached out and met her lips with his own.

Once more Marilyn melted into him, kissing him with all the passion that was in her. They clung together for a moment, then Hunter reluctantly broke away. "I think that Doris is in bed, but you can't ever tell," he said as he turned to get out of the car. He walked Marilyn to the door and gave her one more hard, sweet kiss, then pushed her into the door and shut it behind her, waving good-bye to her shadowy figure in the window as he drove away.

Marilyn sat at her vanity in the bathroom, brushing her hair, a scowl marring her lovely features. What on earth had gotten in to her tonight? What was she thinking of, kissing Hunter like that, and on top of the Tower? Frowning, she gave her hair a vicious jerk and tied it back, then grabbed a bottle of cold cream and started to take off her makeup. *Good grief, Marilyn, you had no business letting the man kiss you like that.* Letting him! That was a joke. She had encouraged him and had certainly met him more than halfway. As she remembered her wanton behavior, her eyes clouded with dismay. *I'm attracted to him,* she thought as guilt washed over her. *I, who have no business being attracted to him, would have been just as happy if he would have gone on kissing me for the rest of the night!*

Disgusted with herself, she snapped off the bathroom light and wandered into her bedroom, throwing back the covers and crawling into bed, pulling the covers up to her chin. *I guess it shouldn't bother me that I'm attracted to him,* Marilyn thought. After all, she'd been divorced for over a year. *But Hunter's a minister,* she wailed inwardly, *and I'm not supposed to be attracted to a minister, at least I don't think I am. But that's ridiculous,* she tried to tell herself. *There's no rule against it, I don't think.*

Marilyn turned over on her side and relived Hunter's devastating embrace, then remembered the first kiss they had shared and jerked herself upright, sitting up in the middle of the bed. *Of course,* she thought, *that's it. He's still trying to break me out of the protective shell he thinks I'm in.* Resentment welled up in Marilyn. *And I guess that he thinks kissing me is the way to go about it. Damn you, Hunter, do you have to interfere in my life? Do you have to play on the attraction that I feel for you? Why don't you just leave me alone?* Marilyn sighed and laid back down, then sat up and set her alarm for an earlier hour, so she could play for Sunday school too.

Hunter lay awake, staring at the ceiling, long after he was usually sound asleep. *What a woman,* he thought. *What a magnificent woman, to respond to him like that.* Hunter sighed, a half-smile on his lips in spite of the frustration he was feeling. He had wanted to go on kissing her, holding her, yes, making love to her, until dawn streaked the skies. It had taken every ounce of strength that he had possessed to pull away from her. Otherwise he would not have been responsible for his actions, and if he had read her right, neither would she. And it wasn't just sex, Hunter thought. She's bright, she's funny, she's great to be with, when she's not grieving for her little boy.

Hunter's smile faded at the thought of Marilyn's child, and he reached up and rubbed his hand across his brow. He was taking a gamble tomorrow by asking Marilyn to play for that class. He had started to tell her everything, but the waiter had brought the salads and he frankly had decided that he better not. Better to spring it on her suddenly and not give her a chance to back out. Hunter frowned into the darkness, anxiety adding to his insomnia. She wasn't going to like it, but tomorrow was the next step in learning to deal with her grief. *And God,* Hunter prayed into the darkness, *please let it work.*

CHAPTER FIVE

Marilyn pushed open the doors to the Sunday school building and peered inside, looking around for Hunter or anyone else who could tell her which Sunday school class she was supposed to play for. She peered down the long corridor, flanked by a row of doors on each side, but did not see anyone who might know where she was supposed to play. Hoping to avoid Hunter, Marilyn wandered down the hall, checking each room, but most of these rooms were used by the adult classes and did not have pianos. Shrugging her shoulders, she retraced her steps and left the building, supposing that she was going to have to face Hunter after all. Her mind burning with the memory of the wild kisses they had shared, Marilyn walked across the breezeway into the church building, heading toward Hunter's office. Why was she letting him interfere in her life the way he was?

She entered the back of the church building and sought out the small pastor's office. She pushed open the door of his office and spotted Hunter in conversation with James McBride, the head elder, a crotchety old soul if there ever was one. Marilyn supposed that there must be a heart buried under all the crust, but she had never seen evidence of it. Nevertheless, she summoned up a smile for both men. "Mr. McBride, Hunter, good morning," she said softly.

Hunter smiled warmly at her, betraying no hint of the intimacy that they had shared the night before except for the sparkle in his eye. "Good morning, Marilyn," he said softly.

"Mrs. Davis," Mr. McBride said, barely nodding his

head as he subtly emphasized the Mrs. Although most of the people in the church had known of her unhappy marriage and had seemed to sympathize when Robert divorced her, Mr. McBride was of the old school who did not believe in divorce, period, in spite of his own daughter's divorce, and he had made his disapproval felt on an occasion or two before. Marilyn usually considered the source and ignored his innuendos, but this morning his attitude rankled her.

"Hunter, I hate to interrupt the two of you, but I don't know where Susan Thomas usually plays, and I'd like to be there on time. Could you tell me where I'm supposed to be?"

"Look, Reverend Templeton," Mr. McBride said, emphasizing the formal title, "I need to be getting along myself. I'll talk to you before church if that's all right."

"Certainly," Hunter said as he turned to Marilyn. "Why don't I take you there?"

"You can just tell me; I don't mind," Marilyn said. "Don't worry about me—I know you're busy."

"It's no trouble," Hunter insisted as he took Marilyn by the arm. "We've moved a lot of the classes in the last six months." Hunter's words were smooth enough, but Marilyn thought she could detect an undertone of tension accompanying them.

Hunter took her by the arm and led her down the back corridor, past the teenage Sunday school classes and into the children's department. Marilyn's eyes darted around suspiciously, then her worst fears were confirmed when Hunter opened the door to Charlene Harrell's class and motioned her inside. Charlene taught the fours and fives, the class that Bobby would have been in if he were alive. She stared in shock at the children, most of whom she knew by name.

Marilyn gasped in pain and horror as she turned to

Hunter with tears in her eyes. "My God, how could you?" she hissed in a pained whisper. "You know this was Bobby's class!" She wrenched her arm away from his and marched toward the door.

Hunter caught up with her as she crossed the walkway and headed for her pickup, grabbing her by the arm and whirling her around. "Marilyn, you said that you'd play for that class. Charlene is depending on you for her singing this morning."

"How cruel can you be?" Marilyn snapped as she tried to shake her arm free, but Hunter's grasp was too tight and she was unable to pull her arm away without making a scene. "You have your nerve, Hunter, asking me to go in there and play for that class. Any other class, even other children, okay. But not those kids. I'm just not ready to face them yet."

Hunter's mouth tightened into a thin strip. "And why not?" he demanded.

"You know damn well why not!" Marilyn shot back, not caring that she was swearing at the minister. "That was Bobby's class, and Bobby would have been in there this morning if he were still alive. You knew that, didn't you?"

"Yes, Marilyn, I knew that. And that's exactly why I asked you to play for them. You simply must start facing Bobby's little friends again, or you're never going to be able to resume your friendships with the people your own age."

"So what is that to you?" Marilyn demanded. "I'm so sick of your interference in my life that I could scream. I was doing just fine until you came along, the do-gooding preacher, just dying to do your bit for the sorrowing of the community. First you drag me back here to play for church, knowing that's going to hurt me, and then you actually have the gall to expect me to go in there and play for those kids! It hurts me just to look at them! Good grief, Hunter, how much do you think I can stand?"

"You can stand a hell of a lot more than you've let yourself," Hunter shot back, unconsciously lapsing into the language of the navy. "You've buried yourself away like an ostrich, not letting yourself heal by facing up to the hurt."

"I know that!" Marilyn cried. "But damn it, that's self-preservation," she added.

"No, it isn't—it's just plain cowardice," Hunter accused her.

Marilyn's head shot up, her eyes narrowing into two angry slits. Hunter had hit on the one thing that Marilyn could not abide. "All right, Hunter Templeton, I'll do it," she said with a cold voice. "Even though I'm not ready. I'll go in there and show you that I'm not a coward, even though it's going to rip my guts out to do it." She turned on her heel and marched into the building, her hands starting to tremble as she drew closer to the Sunday school room.

Hunter watched as the door closed behind her, a frown marring his brow. He honestly had not expected that vehement a response from Marilyn, and her reaction worried him. Maybe she was in fact not ready to face the children. He started to go back, to tell her not to play, but at that moment Hank Schriever came out of the building with a problem that needed his immediate attention. Promising himself that he would check on Marilyn before church, Hunter turned his attention to Hank.

Charlene was waiting for Marilyn with an anxious expression on her face. "Look, Marilyn, I don't think Hunter realized—"

"Yes, he did," Marilyn said tersely. "But it's all right, Charlene, I won't let you down."

"We usually don't sing for a few minutes," Charlene said quietly. "Would you like to come back?"

"That's all right, I'll wait," Marilyn said, sitting in one of the little chairs and watching the children in spite of herself. They were a noisy, happy bunch, and unlike Ryan Bohannon they were all considerably bigger than they had been when she had seen them last. Tears stung her eyes as she watched them play, then Charlene called them together and sat them around a low table. They obediently sat in a wiggling circle and listened with varying degrees of attention as Charlene told them the story of the good Samaritan.

Marilyn sat dully, her heart encased in a cocoon of pain as she watched the little ones listening to the age-old parable, and with Charlene's guidance suggesting ways that they too could be good Samaritans. *They're growing spiritually,* she thought, *as well as in every other way.* Grief throbbed through her as she reflected that Bobby had been deprived of that.

Finally Charlene led the children to sit in a circle around the large piano. Marilyn sat at the bench and turned to Charlene. "How about 'Praise Him, Praise Him'?" Charlene asked.

Marilyn played a bar, then Charlene and the children started into the verse. Marilyn's hands shook and it was all she could do to hit the right keys, in spite of the simplicity of the piece. This was not going to be like the first morning back in the sanctuary, she realized, when the musician in her had taken over. This was simply too close to her grief. She stumbled through the song, shutting her mind to the piping voices singing praise.

Noting Marilyn's distress, Charlene hurried the children through two more songs, then Marilyn started to get up and go before her composure was gone completely, but at that moment Ryan Bohannon, who had made it this morning after all, raised his hand. "Can we sing 'Jesus Loves Me'?" he asked plaintively. "That's my favorite."

The rest of the children chimed in with "Favorite!" "I like it best!" Shrugging, Marilyn sat back down to the piano, tears streaming down her face, her fingers moving over the keys automatically as the little children sang the song that they had played at Bobby's funeral.

As soon as the children had finished, she leaped from the bench and ran from the room, fleeing the tormenting pain. Her vision clouded by tears, she stumbled twice in the hall, then looked around anxiously for a place where she could be alone for a few moments. She spotted the open door to Hunter's office and slipped inside, discovering to her relief that it was empty. She shut the door and sank down on the faded plaid sofa, giving in to harsh, racking sobs that shook her entire body. Long minutes passed as Marilyn gave vent to her grief. Torn by sobs, she did not even hear the door open and Hunter walk inside, shutting the door behind him.

Marilyn jumped as she felt a gentle hand on the back of her neck, then she let herself be guided into Hunter's arms, where fresh tears wet his coat and his shirt front. Hunter slid his other arm around her and let her cry, bitterly cursing himself for thinking that she was ready to face Bobby's class. As Marilyn's sobs subsided, she looked up at him with pain-wracked eyes. "I did it," she whispered. "But please don't ask me to do it again."

Hunter gathered Marilyn close and stroked her back gently. "I'm sorry, hon, I really am," he said softly. "I honestly thought you were ready to face the children."

Marilyn shook her head. "I might have been all right," she sniffed, "but Ryan wanted to sing 'Jesus Loves Me,' and that was the song they sang for Bobby."

"Oh, Marilyn, I'm sorry," Hunter said with contrition.

"I didn't realize." He held her close as her sobbing subsided.

The door flew open suddenly and James McBride strode through it, his eyes widening as he took in the sight of Hunter and Marilyn on the sofa, Hunter's arm around her shoulders. "Well, I do hope I'm not interrupting anything with Mrs. Davis," the old man said sourly, snapping the Mrs. like a pistol shot.

Marilyn sat up and tried to move away, her tear-ravaged face startling Mr. McBride, but Hunter held her close and turned smoldering black eyes onto the old man, although his answer was mild enough. "Well, it seems that you did. I made the mistake of upsetting Marilyn horribly this morning, and I was merely trying to comfort her before she has to go and play for the services."

Mr. McBride sniffed. "Well, that's all well and good, but I wonder if all your women members are comforted so personally?" he asked acidly.

Hunter's anger erupted suddenly. "Why don't you send your own divorced daughter around and find out?" he jibed.

Marilyn gasped at the cruel taunt and Mr. McBride turned pale. Hunter quickly stood up and grasped the old man by the shoulders. "Mr. McBride, I'm sorry. That remark was uncalled for, but I was angered by the nasty crack about Marilyn," he added honestly. "You and everyone else in town know that she did everything that she could to keep that marriage together."

Mr. McBride's shoulders sagged. "You're right, Reverend Templeton. People who live in glass houses shouldn't throw stones. Marilyn, I'm sorry." He looked from Hunter to Marilyn speculatively. "See you both later," he added as he walked out and shut the door behind him.

"Remind me never to make you mad," Marilyn whistled with relief as Hunter let out the breath he had been holding. "You go for the jugular."

"I've spent a lot of time repenting for that particular sin," Hunter admitted as he turned to her anxiously. "Are you all right?" he asked.

Marilyn shrugged. "I hope you don't expect me to play for that class again," she said flatly.

"No," Hunter said quietly. "I should have listened to you. I'm sorry. Do you think you will ever be able to face those children again?"

"Of course," Marilyn said quietly. "But not now. Not yet. I still need more time. But thank you for what you tried to do."

"Don't thank me," Hunter said grimly. "Will you be able to pull yourself together enough to play for the service?"

Marilyn nodded. "I'm thirsty," she said as she opened the door and wandered toward the water fountain at the end of the corridor. Hunter watched her go with a sinking feeling in his stomach, wishing desperately that he had done things differently this morning.

Marilyn walked up to the organ and turned it on, the ravages of her tears repaired as best she could in the restroom. She opened her music and began the soft prelude music, trying to ignore the muted whispering that had accompanied her appearance in the sanctuary. *Thank you, Mr. McBride,* she thought sourly, knowing that her tearstains were not visible to most of the congregation and that Mr. McBride must have told someone what had happened in Hunter's office. Marilyn played through the piece three times, ignoring the stares and the whispers, refusing to look out into the congregation, although most mornings she peeked occasionally to see if the church was filling up. Finally, much to Marilyn's relief, the choir filed in, Hunter behind them, and the service began with a solemn rendition of "A Mighty Fortress Is Our God." The congregation joined in the singing enthusiastically, but many of them eyed either Marilyn or Hunter or both of them speculatively during the morning's announcements. She resolutely ignored the stares she received during the offertory and the special music, and sank into her chair gratefully, her anger at the behavior of the congregation growing by the minute.

How is poor Hunter taking it? she wondered about halfway through the sermon. For if the congregation's scrutiny of her had been thorough, they were observing poor Hunter even more carefully, their eyes narrowed as though in judgment of their new minister. Mr. McBride did his dirty work well, Marilyn thought bitterly as one of the Harrison sisters leaned over and whispered something to her twin, both grinning maliciously. Damn them, what right do they have to say anything, anything at all about Hunter! He's done nothing wrong, nothing at all. Hunter preached with his usual calm assurance, not seeming to notice the attitude of his congregation, although Marilyn could have cheerfully strangled the entire churchful of people.

Finally the service came to an end and Marilyn quickly shed her robe and fled out the back door, hoping to escape the curious eyes of the congregation. *Poor Hunter, having to face that crowd alone,* she thought. *He can't get away like I can.* She took the long way home, her hands trembling in anger as she clutched the steering wheel tightly, pretending that it was sour old Mr. McBride's skinny neck. *Damn him, did he have to tell it all over the church,* she wailed inwardly, then realized that he would not have had to tell the whole church. A couple of people who would tell a couple of others, and that was all it would take. Marilyn tried to tell herself that most of the congregation would understand and think nothing of it, but she could not convince herself that a few would not try to make trouble for Hunter.

Marilyn shed her clothes and made herself a peanut butter sandwich for lunch, but anger robbed her of her appetite and she finally threw most of it into the trash. She was just putting her paper plate in the wastepaper basket when the telephone rang. Expecting a call from her mother, Marilyn was frankly surprised to hear Hunter's voice on the other end of the line. "How are you doing, Marilyn?" he asked quietly. Marilyn could imagine his eyes caressing her with concern in them.

"I'm doing a slow burn," she replied honestly. "Can you believe the way that bunch up there acted this morning? I'd dearly love to strangle every one of them!"

"And you said I was nasty when I got mad!" Hunter laughed into the receiver. "Look, Marilyn, I saw the look on your face during the benediction and I figured you might be feeling this way. I apologize for the way the congregation acted this morning. I know what happened will make you the subject of more gossip, and I'd do anything if I could take back everything I let happen today."

"Well, don't worry about me as far as the gossip goes," Marilyn replied sincerely. "I've been the subject of so much gossip in the past year and a half that I'm getting to be a bore, even to Doris. But what burns me up, Hunter, is the way they're treating you. They're being narrow and very unfair to both of us, really, but you're the one who's going to be hurt in the long run, not me. And that makes me so mad that I could spit!" Marilyn's voice rose until it fairly quivered with indignation.

"I knew there was a reason I didn't come over there and do this in person," Hunter said dryly.

"Oh, Hunter, get serious," Marilyn snapped. "They're

going to chew you up and spit you out in little pieces, and there's not one damned thing we can do to stop them! Oooh, I could just—"

"Now, Marilyn," Hunter chided, "remember that murder's an act of the heart!" In spite of her anger she laughed with him. "But seriously, please don't worry about me and the gossip. People always put their minister up on a pedestal and expect him to stay there. When they find out that we have faults just like they do, they're disappointed. They think that, because we're called by God, we get a little extra dose of holiness, and I can assure you that we don't."

"But how will it affect you and your ministry?" Marilyn asked with real concern.

"Well, as far as the temper goes, I would have blown up at someone sooner or later, and maybe it was better sooner and to someone like James McBride, who is thick-skinned enough to take care of himself."

"And about the insinuations about me?" Marilyn asked softly.

Hunter sighed over the wire. "I just don't know," he said quietly, revealing his own anxiety for the first time. "I simply do not know."

"Well, Boyd says that I absolutely have to work for the next three Sunday mornings to make up for this month," Marilyn said. "So maybe if I'm not around for a few weeks, the gossip will die down some. At least I hope so," she added. "So what will you do? Is Mrs. Weissmann able to play yet?"

"Not really," Hunter said. "But I have a friend who, given a week's notice, might drive down from Austin and do it."

Surprisingly, jealousy flared through Marilyn at the thought of Hunter's friend. "Does she play well?" she asked a bit too casually.

"He's wonderful," Hunter replied, amusement in his

voice at the jealousy she couldn't quite hide. "So again, I'm sorry, and will you try to forgive the church?"

"I'll try," Marilyn promised quietly. "Good-bye, Hunter," she said softly, suddenly bereft at the thought that several weeks could go by before she saw him again.

"Would you like to go out again next Saturday?" Hunter asked quickly before she could hang up.

Joy surged through Marilyn at the invitation, but she sobered quickly. "But if people see us, what will they think?" she asked anxiously. "There will be just that much more gossip."

"Marilyn, if it will make you feel better, next Sunday I'll announce from the pulpit that we're dating but that I don't have any immoral intentions. Now, will you go out with me?" he asked dryly.

"You don't? Aw, shucks," Marilyn said before she could stop herself.

"Seriously, Marilyn, I refuse to let the church dictate my social life. If I want to see you socially, I will, and they can gossip all they like. Is seven all right?"

"Well, if you're sure," Marilyn said hesitantly.

"Positive," Hunter replied firmly. "Only this time wear jeans. See you then!" he replied as he hung up the telephone.

Marilyn sat down on the couch and kicked off her high-heeled shoe, twirling it around her toe absently. "Was that me, defending Hunter like a she-cat?" she whispered, remembering the anger she had felt as she drove home and her vehement words to Hunter in his own defense. Totally astonished at the strength of her feelings of protection toward the compelling minister, she cradled a pillow in her arms and shook her head slowly. *And I still feel indignant,* she thought, remembering the way the congregation had whispered about them both this morning and feeling the anger well up in her again. *Why on earth should I feel this way about Hunter?* she asked herself.

Good question, lady, she thought as she stared out her picture window at the cool, bright afternoon. He had burst into her life with a mission, intending to break her out of the tomb of grief in which she was buried, and to a great extent he had succeeded. This morning had been a mistake on his part, pushing her into something for which she was not quite ready, but for the most part he was succeeding with his mission. She wasn't spending hours anymore brooding about her lost child—she was spending them thinking about Hunter! And he was becoming more, much more to her than just her minister. Marilyn thought about the way his hard body felt against hers when his kissed her, the touch of his sensuous lips on hers, and she longed to be in his arms yet again, to know the sweet delight of his touch. *But I'm just a Christian obligation to him,* she thought morosely. *He's concerned about one of his flock, and he would do the same for anyone in his congregation.* Sighing, Marilyn walked into her bedroom and started dressing to go on duty, thinking wistfully how nice it would be if Hunter came to care for her for herself.

CHAPTER SIX

Marilyn rubbed her weary eyes as she pulled into the driveway and climbed out of the truck. It had been a long day on duty, answering call after call in the cold January drizzle, as accident calls poured in from all over the county. The slick highways and poor visibility had contributed to two major accidents and a number of minor ones, and Marilyn longed for a hot bath and a steaming cup of coffee. She unlocked the door and shut it behind her, stopping long enough to water the beautiful poinsettia that Hunter had brought her for Christmas before she scurried to the bathroom and shed her uniform, filling the tub with hot, cinnamon-scented water. She washed her hair at the basin and slid gratefully into the delicious bath, sinking in up to her neck and letting her mind wander as her body became warm for the first time all day.

Given the chance, her mind wandered to Hunter Templeton, as it often did these days. An unconscious smile played around Marilyn's lips as she remembered the frequent and interesting outings they had gone on in the last six weeks. He had asked her out every Saturday night without fail, changing two invitations to Saturday mornings on the Saturdays she had to work the evening shift. They had eaten at a rustic barbecue place in Fredericksburg and had gone canoeing on Lake Austin. They had driven to San Antonio to do their Christmas shopping, and Hunter had shared the Christmas dinner she had prepared for her parents. Surprisingly, Christmas was not the memory-wracked torture that Marilyn had expected it to be, thanks to Hunter's warm, outgoing nature. He had entertained her parents with many of the same stories that he had told her on the Tower, and Marilyn had to admit that they were just as funny the second time around. And since Christmas they had been to a couple of movies, although after the steamy love scenes in the last one Marilyn wondered if Hunter would want to take her to another. She supposed that people were still gossiping about the two of them, but she enjoyed Hunter's company too much even to care. Sighing, she flicked a soapy washcloth down her arms and legs, hoping for the hundredth time that Hunter would come to like her for herself. Yes, they had shared more of those bone-melting kisses, but in honor of the strong moral code that they both upheld they had very carefully not let things get out of hand.

Marilyn sat up and uttered a mild curse as the telephone rang. She was tempted to stay in the water and let it ring, but she was expecting her mother to call long distance, and it would be a shame to miss her. Hurriedly wrapping herself in a fluffy white towel, she ran, shivering, to the telephone and picked up the receiver.

"Marilyn?" Hunter's tense voice rapped into the receiver before she even had a chance to say hello. "Thank God you're home."

"What is it, Hunter?" Marilyn asked urgently. She had never heard him like this before.

"My car's in the shop, and Suzanne Bohannon desperately needs to get Ryan to San Antonio to the hospital. Can you please take us?"

"Of course," Marilyn replied. "I'll be there in five minutes." She banged down the receiver and raced into jeans and a shirt, skipping makeup and twisting her hair into a wet knot on the back of her neck. She grabbed her coat and raced out the door and not ten minutes later she was parked in front of Suzanne's rambling house. Hunter ran down the sidewalk with Ryan in his arms, the child wrapped in a blanket, and climbed in the front seat beside her. Suzanne climbed in and sat in the jump seat behind Marilyn.

Marilyn glanced over at Ryan as she turned on the ignition and switched on the windshield wipers, then gasped at the sight of the still, blue child. A chilling dread spread through her, the same dread she had felt when she had seen Bobby lying so still in the helicopter wreckage. "What wrong with him?" she asked Hunter through stiff lips.

"His heart," Suzanne volunteered. "He has a serious defect."

Marilyn uttered a rude word that made both Hunter and Suzanne jump. "And it's bad, isn't it?" she asked grimly.

"Yes, it's bad," Suzanne said in a choked voice. "I would have told you, Marilyn, but you've been through so much already," she added. "I knew it would hurt you."

Marilyn nodded wordlessly as she pulled onto the highway and put on her emergency lights. Skillfully, from years of practice at chasing speeders, she wove in and out of the heavy late-afternoon traffic, the heater gradually warming the inside of the truck and the cold knot of wet hair at her neck.

They drove in silence into San Antonio, tension thick in the truck as they battled their way through the steady downpour in pursuit of help for Ryan. Once or twice Marilyn glanced over at the quiet, sick child, his eyelids barely flickering and his breathing labored, and prayed under her breath, "Please, let him be all right, God. Please let him be all right," remembering with despair that she had prayed the same thing for Bobby. *Oh, please, not Ryan too!* she thought as she took the exit to Medical Center Hospital and roared through the city streets, fighting the rush-hour traffic as best she could, until the gigantic hospital loomed before them.

She pulled into the emergency entrance and Hunter immediately leaped from the truck and ran inside with Ryan, Suzanne at his heels. As Marilyn parked the truck, she wondered if in her haste Suzanne had even thought to call Ryan's father in Luling. Jack Bohannon commuted to Luling to work in the oil fields, and sometimes he would be out of touch for hours at a time. As she strode into the hospital, her hands shaking in reaction to the harrowing drive into the city, she spotted a row of telephones in the lobby and stepped up to one. An understanding operator helped her place her call, but Jack was out on a rig and out of immediate reach. Marilyn left word of what had happened, and a concerned young fieldhand said that he would be personally responsible for tracking Jack down and letting him know. Marilyn thanked the fieldhand gratefully and went down the elevator to the emergency room, remembering all too well how to get there. It was the same emergency room they had brought Bobby to.

She found Hunter sitting in one of the plastic chairs that lined the room, one leg crossed over the other, sipping a cup of coffee. Marilyn sat down beside him and accepted a second cup that he handed to her. "I thought you might be ready for this," he said as she sipped the steaming, bitter coffee.

"Yes, I am," Marilyn acknowledged as she swallowed a little of the coffee. "I was going to dry off and have a cup when you called."

Hunter reached up and felt the damp, cold hair on her head. "Good grief, I got you out of the bathtub and dragged you back out in the cold," he said ruefully. "I won't apologize, though, because Ryan needed help."

"Of course," Marilyn said simply. "I knew something had to be wrong that day in the grocery store," she added more to herself than to Hunter. "He was so thin, and he had grown so little since the last time he and Bobby played," she added.

"Did the boys play together often?" Hunter asked.

Marilyn smiled faintly. "All the time," she said. "They used to live at the end of our block." She sipped her coffee and stared into space. "Oh, I wish I'd known about Ryan," she said softly. "Maybe there would have been something I could have done." She reached up and wiped a tear from her eye.

Hunter laid his hand on her arm. "Suzanne has told practically no one about Ryan," he said softly. "I think she didn't want people to feel sorry for them."

"I can understand that," Marilyn replied. "So how much do you know? Or are you under ministerial confidence?"

"No, not in this case," Hunter replied. "Ryan has a congenital defect. The details escape me at the moment, but basically his blood is not getting enough oxygen, and the situation has been getting worse over the last year or so. The doctors are not in agreement as to the best treatment for him, so the Bohannons are afraid to do anything at all."

"I know that feeling too," Marilyn said dryly. Hunter looked at her with surprise. "The doctors argued over whether or not to try a last-ditch operation to save Bobby. We went on with the operation, but it didn't do any good." Abruptly she got up and wandered over to the nurses' station, Hunter following behind her. "Have you any word on the Bohannon boy?" she asked the head nurse, who looked vaguely familiar.

"He's holding his own," the woman said encouragingly, bringing the ghost of a smile to Marilyn's lips. The woman looked at her strangely. "Have you been in here before?" she asked curiously.

Marilyn nodded. "The helicopter crash in New Braunfels a year and a half ago. The little boy."

The woman's face cleared. "Of course, you were his mother. We heard down here that he didn't make it. I'm real sorry."

Marilyn nodded sadly. "I kept hoping right until the last that they would find some way to save him," she said frankly. "But they didn't."

The nurse looked at her compassionately. "I won't say it was for the best, because I know you would have wanted him under any circumstances."

Marilyn looked at the nurse strangely. "Under what circumstances?" she asked with puzzlement. "What do you mean?"

The nurse looked uncomfortable. "You mean the nurses upstairs didn't tell you?" she asked softly. "Even if your child had lived, he would have been hopelessly brain damaged. That clot at the base of the brain had shut off the oxygen supply to most of his cerebrum and cerebellum. He would have been without conscious thought and muscular control." The nurse looked with concern at Marilyn's shocked face. "I'm sorry, maybe I shouldn't have told you."

"No, that's all right," Marilyn said quickly, her shock subsiding a little. "I only wish someone had told me then. It might have hurt a little less."

Hunter slipped his arm around Marilyn comfortingly. "Will you call us as soon as you know anything about Ryan?" he asked the nurse. "We'll be right over there."

"Well, they'll be moving him up to Pediatrics in a few minutes," the nurse volunteered. "I'll see that someone lets you know, so you can go upstairs with him."

Hunter and Marilyn resumed their wait, Marilyn's mind spinning. So even if Bobby had lived, he wouldn't have been her bright, beloved child anymore. He would have had to spend his life as an invalid, a vegetable. Wouldn't that have been worse in the long run, to watch him suffer like that? Marilyn rubbed her head with the palm of her hand, her mind whirling with confusion. She simply did not know.

About half an hour later the nurse informed them that Ryan had been transferred to Pediatric Intensive Care. Remembering the route well, Marilyn delivered Hunter to the proper wing and went in search of a telephone, but the fieldhand still had not been able to locate Jack.

She retraced her steps to the intensive care unit and found Suzanne and Hunter standing just outside Ryan's door, Suzanne's thin shoulders shaking with sobs. Marilyn reached out and gathered her friend to her, letting Suzanne cry her heart out. "Dear God, I didn't know it could hurt so bad. Even when you lost Bobby I didn't know how it hurt," Suzanne sobbed as Marilyn held her comfortingly.

"I'm sorry, Suzanne, that it had to be Ryan," Marilyn crooned, tears spilling out of her eyes. She steered Suzanne to a small couch along one corridor and pushed her down gently. "Now, Suzanne, you have to pull yourself together, for Ryan's sake," she said softly but firmly. "You don't want to be upset like this when you go back in there to him, now, do you?"

"Of course not," Suzanne said as she sniffed and took a deep breath.

Marilyn looked at her watch and discovered that it was after eight. "Suzanne, Hunter, I'm going to go out and get hamburgers for the three of us," she said quietly. "Can I hit you up for a bill, Hunter? I'm flat broke."

"Oh, Marilyn, I couldn't possibly eat," Suzanne said quickly.

"Yes, you can, and you must," Marilyn said firmly. "You may be here for a long haul, Suzanne, and you must keep up your strength for Ryan's sake. So, please, will you eat something if I bring it?"

Suzanne nodded as Hunter handed Marilyn a crumpled ten. She left the hospital and returned half an hour later with a bag of McDonald's hamburgers, which they all did justice to, even Suzanne. Marilyn tried Luling again and learned that Jack had made an unexpected trip to Victoria and was not expected back before eleven or twelve. That would put him here after one, Marilyn thought tiredly, so she called Boyd and had him change her to tomorrow's afternoon shift.

Hunter and Marilyn stayed with Suzanne, not saying much, but supporting her with their presence. Ryan was awake on and off and Suzanne sat by his bed, holding his thin hand in hers. Marilyn and Hunter alternated a little with Suzanne, and Marilyn's heart went out to the small child gasping for breath. Even after he was hurt, Bobby had never looked this bad, and she thought gratefully that her child had never been allowed to suffer as Ryan was doing now.

Jack Bohannon arrived a little after one, and he and Hunter went in together to see Ryan. Both men came out with tears running unashamedly down their cheeks, big redheaded Jack totally helpless to do anything for his son. He sat down on the couch beside his wife and took her hand in his, lifting it to his lips and kissing it gently. "We need to pray for Ryan, hon," he said softly. "Hunter and Marilyn, won't you join us?"

Marveling at the calm in Jack's voice, Marilyn bowed her head. Hunter prayed first, asking Divine healing for Ryan, and strength for Ryan and his parents in the hours and days to come. Then Jack spoke, his voice trembling yet strong as he prayed. "You gave Ryan to us, Lord, when we thought there weren't going to be any more children for us, and we love him with all our hearts. But we know that You love him, too, and have a plan for him. And if that plan is for him to leave us, and be with You, then please help us accept that, and give us the strength to bear it." Jack's voice did not break, but he was obviously too overcome to continue. Suzanne reached out with tears in her eyes and held Jack tightly.

Marilyn wiped her eyes as she gazed at her friends, her awe on her face as she realized what kind of strength and trust that prayer had taken. She had prayed when Bobby was hurt, but her prayers had been a simple plea for Bobby's life. When Bobby had died the praying had stopped, Marilyn feeling that her prayers had not been answered. Yet Jack and Suzanne had expressed their willingness to let their child die, if that was meant to be. She sensed that whatever happened tonight or in the days to come, that Jack's and Suzanne's hearts would be comforted. She looked over at Hunter and saw the same admiration in his eyes for the Bohannons, and wondered if even Hunter's faith was as strong as theirs.

Hunter stood and reached for his overcoat. "Jack, Suzanne, we're going to go. I'll call here before I go to bed and see if there is any change in Ryan, and I'll be back in the morning."

"Thank you," Jack said simply.

"You can use my truck," Marilyn told Hunter. "I'll have Doris run me to work. And Suzanne, I want you to call me if there's anything I can do," she added as she reached out and hugged Suzanne tightly. "I know what you're going through, and if I can do anything to help, then you know I will."

"I will call you," Suzanne promised. "Just having someone to talk to who knows how I feel would be a help."

Marilyn and Hunter walked out to the parking lot in silence, a cold, damp wind blowing in their faces and ruffling Hunter's hair. Marilyn unlocked the driver's side and handed Hunter the keys, then walked around to the other side and waited for Hunter to unlock the door for her. He reached over and popped open the door, then turned on the ignition as Marilyn pulled the door shut behind her and fumbled for the seat belt. "You don't like to drive at night?" he asked as they pulled out of the parking lot.

Marilyn smiled fleetingly as she thought of all the night driving she did as a deputy. "No, I don't mind," she said. "But frankly, I wanted you to drive the truck tonight on the empty roads before you try to drive it up here in the city traffic in the morning. A truck's a little different, you know."

"Yes, I know," Hunter said, a smile playing around his mouth. "I remember how little my Mustang seemed the first time I drove it."

"Oh, you've driven a truck before," Marilyn said as she leaned her head against the headrest. "Oh, well, I'm tired anyway. Did you grow up in the country?"

"Ozarks," Hunter said simply. He fell silent, maneuvering the truck through the sparse late-night traffic. Marilyn sat back, her mind returning to the sick little boy they had left behind, and the almost unbelievable strength that his parents had shown. Marilyn knew without a shadow of a doubt that she did not possess that kind of strength and that she never would. As they drove back to New Braunfels, she found herself wondering for the millionth time why a child like Bobby had to die and why Ryan had to suffer and probably die also. Although she tried to stop herself, she felt the old bitterness over Bobby's death creep over her, compounded by her very real sorrow over little Ryan, and her heart was swamped with confusion. How could such cruel things be allowed to happen, especially to parents such as herself and the Bohannons, who loved their children more than life itself?

Hunter pulled into Marilyn's driveway and killed the engine. "Are you sure about the truck tomorrow?" he asked anxiously. "I wouldn't want to put you out."

Marilyn nodded her head. "Of course," she replied. "When are you going?"

"That depends on how Ryan is doing," Hunter replied. "If his condition remains stable, I won't go until the middle of the morning, but if he—well, if something should happen, I'll of course go immediately. In fact, I need to go home and call the hospital and see how he's doing."

"Why don't you call from the house?" Marilyn suggested. "I'd like to know too."

Hunter nodded and together they walked up the sidewalk to her front door. Marilyn turned up the heater while Hunter made the call from her kitchen telephone. She got out the coffeepot and measured out the coffee, then got out her omelette pan and a carton of eggs. It had been hours since she and Hunter had eaten their hamburgers, and one hamburger wasn't much to keep a man Hunter's size going.

As she cracked eggs into a mixing bowl and beat them, Hunter hung up the telephone and turned around to her. "No change yet, so I said I'd call them as soon as I woke up in the morning. Say, what are you making?" he asked, coming to peer over her shoulder.

"Coffee and omelettes, and I'm making some for you. You're bound to be hungry after all this time," Marilyn replied as she grated up a little cheese to go in the eggs.

"That would be great," Hunter replied fervently. "I've never mastered an omelette."

"I'd offer to teach you, but I'm just plain too tired," Marilyn admitted. "Some other time."

"Julia Child, I accept," Hunter said as he reached down and kissed her cheek gently. "But shouldn't you be getting on to bed? You have to go to work in the morning."

"I called from the hospital and got changed to the afternoon shift," Marilyn said as she poured the eggs into the omelette pan. "I figured we would be there awhile."

She let the eggs cook until they were just right, then expertly flipped them, letting them cook a moment longer. Hunter got out a jug of milk and rummaged around until he found knives and forks, then he set the table and poured the milk and coffee while Marilyn cooked the second omelette. They sat down at her kitchen table and dug into the omelettes like two starving prisoners eating their first meal in a month. They talked little until the omelettes were gone, then Hunter drained his milk glass and asked for another.

Marilyn poured it and handed it to him, laughing at the milk moustache that appeared on his upper lip. "You have a milk moustache just like Bobby's," she said laughingly, then sobered at the mention of her son.

"Little boys have a way of getting those," Hunter said lightly, watching Marilyn's face cloud.

"Ryan gets them too," Marilyn said absently.

Abruptly she got up and put her dishes in the sink, the bitterness that she had felt on the way home welling up in her as she remembered her own son, and the child who was lying in that hospital bed in San Antonio. She put the milk carton into the refrigerator and took Hunter's plate to the sink, then she sat down across from Hunter again, her face bleak. "It just doesn't seem fair," she said softly. "Ryan's only four."

"His parents' strength is something to see, isn't it?" Hunter said quietly. "I don't see that too often in my ministry. To be willing to let go of a child like that—well, that's rare."

"Yes, it is," Marilyn agreed grimly. "You sure wouldn't have seen that around here. I'm certainly not capable of that."

"Not too many of us are," Hunter said. "It takes someone very special to say what they said tonight and mean it."

"But it's unfair!" Marilyn said bitterly, her control over her emotions breaking. "Why should parents even have to say that? Why should they have to let their children go? Why does an innocent little kid like Bobby have to die, and a child like Ryan lay there and suffer? Why, Hunter, why?"

"Good grief, Marilyn, I don't know why!" Hunter exploded, jumping up and striding back and forth across her small kitchen. "You think I have all the answers? You think I have a hotline to heaven for all the explanations? How do you think I felt sitting there tonight, with one woman who has lost a beloved child and another who's probably going to, not having a single thing I can say to explain any of it to either one of you. Don't you think I've wondered the same thing, every time I'm called to the hospital to sit with the parents of a small child, or have to preach the funeral of a father of three who was killed by a drunk driver, or visit with a forty-year-old who's so crippled by arthritis that she's in a wheelchair? Don't you think I've asked my share of whys?"

"You have?" Marilyn asked incredulously as she stared up into Hunter's anguished eyes.

Hunter nodded. "Let me tell you about it," he said as he took her hand and led her to the living room. He sat her down on the living room couch and held her hand in his. "Yes, I have doubts sometimes," he admitted honestly. "I ask the same questions that you do sometimes, perhaps more often than most people because my congregation always expects me to have all the answers. They come to me with questions the same as yours—why did I lose my child, or why am I sick, why am I out of work, and, yes, I wonder how God could allow that. Sometimes

I can see maybe a glimpse of a plan, but at other times it makes no sense to me either."

"I know," Marilyn said. "That's how I feel about Bobby, or did until tonight. I could never have prayed the way Jack did for him and Suzanne. Could you?"

"I'm not sure," Hunter admitted. "I've never had a child, so I can't appreciate the depth of feeling that a parent has for one. Tell me, did talking with the nurse tonight change your feelings about losing Bobby?"

"I don't know," Marilyn admitted. "I wouldn't have wanted to lose Bobby under any circumstances. But then again, I wouldn't have wanted him to be a vegetable either. There are some things that are worse than death, and that may be one of them."

"That's true," Hunter said frankly. "So we come up with another no-answer situation. Oh, Marilyn, believe me, I wish I had all the answers for you and all the others out there who have been hurt. And it seems like it's always someone like you, who never did anything to anybody. But I don't, and I probably never will. Hey," he added softly, "I'm sorry I blew up at you like I did. That was the last thing you needed."

"It's okay," Marilyn reassured him gently, reaching up and caressing his face with her hand. "I guess you needed to let off steam, and so did I. It's just that I felt so bitter watching Ryan suffer like that. And then it brought it all back about Bobby. I begged and pleaded with God to let my child live, and then Bobby didn't make it."

"Tell me, did you pray after he was gone?" Hunter asked quietly.

"No," Marilyn replied baldly. "There didn't seem much point. I know that after what we saw tonight I sound terrible, and I guess I was. But I just wasn't ready to let Bobby go. It was too sudden."

"Well, it's true that Jack and Suzanne have had a lot

more time than you did to prepare themselves for the possibility of Ryan's death. But how about later? After Bobby was gone, how did you react? How do you feel now?"

"Frankly, I couldn't believe it for months," Marilyn replied honestly. "I kept expecting to get a telegram from heaven saying there had been a mistake, or for Bobby to walk through that door. Then, when it finally sank in that he was really gone, I was angry. I'm still angry when I stop and think about it. I just wasn't ready to let him go!"

"Did you ever let him go, Marilyn?" Hunter asked gently.

Marilyn shook her head slowly. "No, I didn't. I still haven't," she added as she turned to him, his eyes shining with tears. "I've never been able to believe that Bobby is somewhere else now. I still think he should be here with me."

"How about your husband?" Hunter asked gently. "Sometimes people will refuse to let go emotionally after a divorce too. Are you grieving for Robert too?"

"I can't let go of something I never held," Marilyn replied softly. "I never really could call Robert mine, and after the first few months the only reason we stayed together was for Bobby. Maybe that's why losing Bobby hurt so much," she added wisely. "I had poured all my love into my child, knowing that I could never love his father or be loved by him the way that I needed."

"So where will you go from here?" Hunter prompted her gently.

A grim smile played around Marilyn's lips. "I guess the next step should be to tell you that I'm ready to let go of Bobby the way the Bohannons did their child tonight. But I can't do that just yet."

"Because you will never understand that kind of tragedy?" Hunter asked softly.

Marilyn shook her head. "I doubt that Jack and Suzanne understand either. No, I'm just not ready to admit that Bobby doesn't belong with me anymore. I know I'm going to have to, though, before I can get on with my life. But Hunter, how can I do that?"

"Again, I don't have all the answers," Hunter said as they both nodded. "But tell me, what do you do when you feel a memory of Bobby coming on?"

"I shut it off as quickly as I can, or I try to," Marilyn admitted honestly. "Remembering is so painful!"

"Tell me, if Ryan dies, do you think that Jack and Suzanne will shut off those memories?"

"Probably not," Marilyn admitted. "They'll treasure Ryan's memory."

"Maybe you should start by doing just that. I asked you once a long time ago to tell me about Bobby, and you shut me off. Don't shut me off tonight. Tell me about Bobby."

So Marilyn did. Haltingly at first, then in a torrent of words she remembered her son to Hunter, telling him about her pregnancy, Bobby's birth, his early days, about all the cute little things he had said and done, about the time he had shoved a pear down the toilet and clogged it up, and about the time he asked why a baldheaded friend had a shiny head. She remembered how he would roll across the floor before he could even walk and teethe on the coffee table, and how he had stomped out the bottom of the playpen one day when she wouldn't take him out of it. As she talked and then got out the picture albums, she unconsciously drew Hunter a picture not only of Bobby, but of the mother that she had been, and he began to comprehend for the first time the magnitude of her loss. For the first time he could understand the desolation of her grief and why she was having such a hard time getting over her son's death, and he admired her for the progress that she had made.

Marilyn snapped shut the last of the picture albums and turned to Hunter. "That's all," she said softly. "The accident was just a few days later."

"Tell me, Marilyn, now that you've talked about him, do you think you're any closer to letting go of your son?" Hunter asked quietly.

"I think so," Marilyn admitted, "but I haven't done it yet. I will try, Hunter," she promised him sincerely. She glanced down at her watch and gasped. "Oh, no, it's after six!" she yelped. "It's almost morning!"

"It is morning," Hunter said softly.

"Oh, Hunter, you should have stopped me," Marilyn protested. "I talked for three hours! You won't get any sleep at all."

"Now, don't go worrying about my sleep," Hunter admonished her gently. "You needed to talk about Bobby, and I was more than glad to listen. I do need to go now though," he said as he pulled Marilyn close to him. "Thank you for understanding what it's like for me," he added softly.

"Thank you for understanding what it's like for me," Marilyn replied. "I'm glad you don't have all the answers either."

Hunter pulled Marilyn close and held her tightly, then tipped her face up to his. "I know it's late, but I need to touch you for just a few minutes after all we've shared tonight," he said as he reached down and claimed her lips with his own.

This kiss was not like all the other passion-filled kisses that Marilyn and Hunter had shared in the last few weeks. Before, they had reached out to each other with wild passion, fighting the urge to abandon their scruples and make uninhibited love. But tonight Marilyn sensed that this kiss and caress could go on for hours without either of them being forced to pull away. It was a comforting caress, a communication as much of hearts as of bodies. Hunter explored her mouth gently with his lips and his tongue, holding her securely in the crook of his arm while he leisurely stroked the small of her back with his hand. Marilyn's hands lightly stroked his waist, finding comfort in the hard warmth of Hunter's body, then her arms crept upward and curled around the secure warmth of his chest. She snuggled closer to him, wanting to draw closer to the mind and the spirit of Hunter, to draw from his strength and share with him of hers.

Hunter drew his lips away from hers and leisurely explored her face and her neck with his tender mouth, and in spite of the nature of their embrace he trailed his hand down her shirt front and found one of her breasts under her shirt, stroking the nipple until it became taut in his hand. He reached out and opened the top buttons of her shirt and slowly slid his hand inside, finding and touching her other nipple gently until it, too, was hard. Marilyn unconsciously thrust her body toward his enticing fingers, wanting to prolong the exquisite sensations he was arousing in her with his touch. Daringly she reached up and placed the flat of her hand to his heart, surprised to find that it was beating even faster than her own. Hunter drew his hand away from her breast but pulled her to him, taking her lips with a force that took her breath away. Mindlessly she clung to him, whimpering a little in protest as he slowly drew his mouth from hers, then he crushed her to his chest, holding her head close to his heart.

"I guess I better go," Hunter said hoarsely as he finally pulled away.

Marilyn nodded as Hunter fumbled with her buttons. Shyly, remembering the wanton way that she had responded to his touch, she pushed away his clumsy fingers and buttoned up her shirt. "Call me when you find out anything about Ryan," she said softly. "If it's after three, call the sheriff's office and have them radio me the message. Do you have the truck keys?" she asked.

Hunter nodded and propelled himself off the couch, pulling Marilyn up with him and walking with her to the door. He kissed her once more slowly before he strode down the sidewalk and got into her truck, disappearing into the early morning gloom. Marilyn watched him go, a bemused smile on her face, too tired to even think about what she and Hunter had accomplished tonight. She took a quick shower and tumbled into bed, falling into a deep sleep, dreaming of the touch of Hunter's lips on hers.

Hunter rubbed his sleepy eyes and squinted at the clock on the dashboard. The clock read almost noon, so he figured that he must have gotten about four hours sleep, not enough after staying up all night with the Bohannons and Marilyn, but he guessed that it would have to do.

As he took the turnoff into San Antonio, he remembered the way that Marilyn had clung to him and responded to his kisses. It took every ounce of his self-control to keep from turning the truck around and driving straight back to New Braunfels and Marilyn's tender arms. What had he been missing all these years? Suddenly his deep devotion to God and his congregation, which had been all the love that he had needed for years, simply wasn't enough anymore. Hunter realized with surprise that he wanted the love of a woman in his life. For years he had grimly thrust aside the possibility of a helpmate, convinced after his fiancée had left him that he wanted no part of love and marriage for himself, but now he was not so sure. Marilyn had awakened not only his physical desires, but his deep longing for an emotional bond with a woman.

Thrusting thoughts of his own needs away, Hunter thought about Marilyn as he jockeyed her huge truck through the heavy city traffic. She had done so well yesterday. She had not only reached out to Suzanne with the special compassion of one who has known similar sorrow, but she had turned to him with the same understanding and sympathy for his frustration. And then she had talked about her son for the first time, and had not seemed to be saddened by bringing the child to mind. *You're getting there, Marilyn,* he thought happily. *You're going to get over the grief, I just know you will.* Hunter smiled to himself as he pulled into the hospital parking lot. He was sure that very soon Marilyn was going to be all right.

Marilyn walked across the street and up Doris's sidewalk, raising her knuckles to knock on the front door. Before she could knock, however, Doris had thrown open the door and was motioning Marilyn inside. "Do you have time for a cup of hot chocolate before I drive you down to the office?" Doris asked eagerly.

"Sounds delicious," Marilyn replied sincerely as she tossed her hat on Doris's coffee table. "I'd love one." She followed Doris to her cheerful kitchen and gratefully accepted a mug of rich, steaming chocolate, then sat down at Doris's kitchen table. "Doris, you have to make the best cup of chocolate in New Braunfels."

Doris beamed. "I'm glad you like it," she said delightedly.

Marilyn sipped her chocolate eagerly, only burning her mouth a little on the hot liquid. "Doris, I sure appreciate you taking me to work like this. I doubt that Hunter will be back before night."

"And how is that precious little child?" Doris asked with real concern in her voice.

"Hunter said that Ryan had rallied this morning and was actually doing better. Frankly, the poor little fellow needs all the help he can get to get well," Marilyn said honestly. Normally Marilyn was a little guarded in what she said to Doris, but Ryan's condition was no secret, and all of the Sunday school classes had put him on their prayer list early this morning.

"Well, I think it's just wonderful that you're helping Hunter with his ministerial duties now and not waiting until after your wedding," Doris said beamingly.

Marilyn choked on a mouthful of chocolate. "What wedding?" she asked in shock.

"Why, yours and the preacher's, of course," Doris said serenely. "You're engaged, aren't you?"

"Good grief, where did you get an idea like that?" Marilyn sputtered. "We most certainly aren't engaged!"

Doris's face fell. "Why, I thought sure you were engaged. He's over by you all the time, and you lent him your truck today."

"Hunter takes me out once a week or so," Marilyn replied patiently. "Nothing serious. And under the circumstances I would have lent my truck to anyone."

"But I saw him leaving your house early this morning," Doris said innocently. "I told Evelyn Jennings that I bet he went by there for breakfast before he left for San Antonio."

Marilyn groaned inwardly and slumped in her seat. Although Doris was an inveterate gossip, she would put the most innocent interpretation on seeing Hunter leave Marilyn's at six in the morning. Evelyn, however, could worm an X rating out of *Mary Poppins,* and she would be sure to put the most damning interpretation on what Doris had told her, especially when word got around that she and Hunter had left the hospital about one and that her pickup truck had sat in the driveway of the parsonage until almost noon. Damn! Couldn't Doris keep her mouth shut? Drinking her chocolate, Marilyn wondered tiredly what this latest spate of gossip would do to Hunter's effectiveness in the church. Although their "night" together had been entirely innocent, it wouldn't stay that way very long in the mouths of New Braunfels's gossip mill.

"Anyway, I wouldn't be surprised if Hunter pops the question to you before too long, Marilyn," Doris said confidently, her round face beaming with imagined delight. "Oh, a wedding on the block! I can hardly wait!"

Marilyn laughed. "Well, as of now, Doris, there is no wedding in the offing. But I'll make you a deal. If Hunter proposes and I accept, you'll be the first to know." *And that would save me the cost of announcements,* she added wickedly to herself. Doris nodded her agreement, and the conversation turned to other matters.

But wouldn't it be nice if Doris were right? Marilyn asked herself later as she cruised the farm-to-market road that circled Canyon Lake. She and Hunter, sharing breakfast in the morning, reading a book together after supper, making love in that big corner bedroom in the parsonage. Totally shocked when she realized where her thoughts had led her, Marilyn pulled over to the side of the road and held her head in her hands. What on earth was she thinking of? She and Hunter married? The idea was ridiculous. Hunter did not love her. She was just a Christian obligation to him and nothing more. And what was he to her? A minister helping her overcome her grief? That was what he was supposed to be.

But he had become much more to her than that, Marilyn realized with despair as she stared out at the sunset over the lake, the red and orange light reflecting from the lake's surface with molten splendor. She loved him. She had fallen in love with Hunter Templeton, although that was the last thing she had wanted to do. "Oh, damn!" Marilyn said out loud in the empty patrol car. "That's all I need." She stared out into the setting sun until her eyes watered, her heart sore over the discovery she had made.

She did not want to love Hunter. Loving meant hurting, and she had hurt enough. Besides, he did not love her. She was only a part of what he considered his ministerial duties, although she had enough sense to know that he had not kissed her entirely in the line of duty.

Yes, she loved Hunter, she acknowledged to herself, and although one part of her recoiled at that thought, the other part of her wished Doris's silly speculations were true. She wished that Hunter would ask her to marry him, and that she could live with him and help him with his duties. She sighed as she switched on the engine and pulled out on the road. She was in love, but her love had no future. As she reached down to answer a call, she wondered sadly why it was that she, who had already known so much sadness in her short life, seemed destined to know even more.

CHAPTER SEVEN

Marilyn parked the squad car and wandered into the sheriff's office, whistling under her breath. Thank goodness that shift was over! She would go out to eat a very early breakfast with Tess and then she would tumble into bed for a few hours of sleep before she got ready for her date with Hunter. Eagerly anticipating her Saturday night date with him, Marilyn opened the door and walked inside, noticing that the trio of deputies in the corner glanced toward her furtively and became very quiet for a moment. *What's with them?* she wondered as she gave her car keys to Boyd and sat down to do her paperwork. She only had a few forms to fill out, and before long she handed them to Boyd and motioned to Tess across the room. Tess nodded and picked up her hat, and the two of them walked out to Tess's car. "I really appreciate the transportation this week," Marilyn said as Tess unlocked the car door and let her in.

"Glad to help out," Tess said as she got in on her side and started the engine. "How much longer is Hunter going to need your truck?"

"His car will be out of the shop tomorrow," Marilyn replied, "and they sent Ryan Bohannon home today, so Hunter wouldn't have had to run back and forth to San Antonio anymore, anyway."

"How is Ryan?" Tess asked softly.

"Not so good," Marilyn admitted sadly. "He's had a reprieve, that's all. The doctors were not at all encouraging."

"Damn," Tess said succinctly as she pulled into the small coffee shop that was just opening its doors to early-morning customers. Tess and Marilyn sat in a booth and ordered large plates of eggs and sausages, since they hadn't eaten for nine hours or better. Marilyn noticed that the waitress looked at her a little strangely as she put her plate in front of her.

"I wonder what's with her?" Marilyn said out loud as she dug into her eggs. "She looked at me like I had three heads."

Tess looked uncomfortable and mumbled something under her breath. "What was that?" Marilyn asked as she cut her sausage with her fork.

"Oh, nothing," Tess replied, although from the look on her face there was definitely something wrong.

Marilyn eyed Tess with narrowed eyes. "Come on out with it, Tess," Marilyn demanded. "Why did she look at me that way?"

"I guess it's the gossip," Tess said as she swallowed a bite of toast.

"About the gay divorcée and the minister?" Marilyn asked softly.

Tess nodded miserably. "It's all over town that he spent the night at your house. Doris Bettencourt said she saw him leave at six in the morning."

"He left at six fifteen," Marilyn corrected her as Tess choked on her coffee.

"What? You mean he really spent the night there? Marilyn, what on earth?"

Marilyn shook her head disgustedly. "Yes, he really spent the night there," she said. "If I tell you what actually happened, will you believe me?"

"Well-l-l," Tess shrugged.

"See what I mean?" Marilyn snapped irritably. "Even you drew the wrong conclusion, and you're my best friend. The night was totally innocent, but maybe about one person in a hundred will believe that. Damn! I don't care for myself, but it's going to wreck everything Hunter has worked to achieve in the church."

"What did happen?" Tess asked softly.

"We were late coming back from San Antonio and the Bohannons. I cooked him an omelette, and we got to talking about Ryan and all the unfair things that seem to happen to nice people. One thing led to another and I spent three hours telling him about Bobby."

Tess smiled faintly. "The man must be something if he got you to do that," she said softly. "But unfortunately, if the gossip keeps up, his reputation is going to be mud."

"Do you suppose Hunter is aware of what's being said?" Marilyn asked anxiously.

Tess shrugged. "Are you going to say anything to him?" she asked.

Marilyn looked at her friend morosely. "I guess I'll have to," she said as the waitress brought them their check. Marilyn pushed her half-eaten food away and picked up the check. "My treat," she said as she walked toward the cash register, her shoulders slumping dejectedly.

Marilyn went home and fell into a deep sleep, exhaustion claiming her in spite of the turmoil she felt over the gossip. She woke up late in the afternoon and had to rush through a shower to be ready for Hunter. In fact, she had not quite finished blowing her hair dry when the doorbell rang and she ran to let Hunter in, irritation over her own tardiness compounded with the news about the gossip making her cross.

"Come in," she scowled as she ran back toward the bathroom, her robe flopping around her ankles and her half-wet hair flying in all directions. Her good humor was not restored by the sound of Hunter's laughter echoing through the living room.

Marilyn dried her hair and pulled on a purple velvet

dress, applying her makeup quickly but skillfully, and finding a pair of black pumps. Hunter had told her that they were going into San Antonio for dinner, and she thought that the purple would look nice in any of the big-city restaurants. She bit her lip as she transferred her wallet and her brush into her dress purse. How would Hunter react to the news about the gossip? Would he stop seeing her in order to protect his career? Involuntarily Marilyn shied away from that solution to his problem. Her life would be so empty if Hunter were not in it. How would she bear it, being cut off from the man she loved? But what could he do? Ignore the ugly lies that were spreading about them?

Hunter and Marilyn made small talk on the way into San Antonio and through a delicious seafood dinner, Marilyn's mind only half on their conversation, the other half on Hunter's probable reaction to her news about the gossip. She skipped dessert and ordered a coffee, postponing her unpleasant task as long as possible, her fingers nervously knotting the napkin in her lap.

As Hunter took the last bite of his strawberry shortcake, he stared at her with his piercing black eyes. "Out with it," he demanded.

"Huh?" Marilyn asked, caught off-guard.

"I said, out with it. Whatever's got you so tied up in knots that you can't tell me. Have you decided that you don't want to see me anymore?" he demanded, his face strained.

"Oh, no, not that!" Marilyn blurted out quickly. "But you may not want to see me again when you hear what the problem is," she said sadly.

Hunter's face cleared. "I doubt that," he said softly. "So what is getting to you so badly then?" he asked, coaxing Marilyn to speak.

"It's all over New Braunfels that you spent the night at

my house," Marilyn said baldly. "Even Tess said she wondered what went on."

The strain instantly reappeared on Hunter's face. "I knew there had been some talk, but I had no idea that it was that vicious. Did you tell Tess the truth?"

"Yes, I told her and she believed me. But how many others would, do you think?"

"A small minority," Hunter admitted heavily. "The rest would be convinced that either I was seduced by that young divorcée or that their innocent Marilyn has been compromised by a veteran womanizer taking advantage of his position as a minister."

Marilyn winced at the bitterness in his tone. "Have you ever been the victim of this kind of gossip?" she asked.

Hunter shook his head. "No, never," he admitted. "I guess I left us both wide open that night by not leaving earlier, but I never dreamed anyone would see me leave so early in the morning."

"Hunter, is there anything we can do? Maybe if you just got up and explained in church what really happened?" she offered weakly.

"And dignify their horrible tattling?" Hunter asked bitingly. "Besides, it would only do more damage. No, Marilyn, there's not one thing that either one of us can do about it. I guess I've dragged you through the gossip mill again."

"For heaven's sake, don't worry about me," Marilyn said firmly. "It's your ministry I'm worried about."

"I'm worried about it too," Hunter admitted as the waiter brought him the check.

"Hunter, I hate to bring this up, but there's one very effective way you could quell the gossip," Marilyn said quietly. "If you stopped seeing me, the gossip would die down."

"Is that what you want?" Hunter asked her through lowered lids.

"No," Marilyn replied frankly. "I wouldn't like it one bit. But you have your career to consider. It would be foolish to throw away everything you've worked for by continuing to see me."

Hunter picked up the check, and together they walked toward the cash register. He paid for the meal and they left the restaurant, not speaking until they were sitting in the cab of the truck. Then he reached over and slowly drew Marilyn across the seat until she was sitting close to him and slid his arm around her shoulders. "No, Marilyn, I'm not going to stop seeing you. I don't want that, and neither do you. I don't know what to do about the gossip, but sacrificing my friendship with you is not on my list of solutions. Do you understand?" he continued as he reached down and kissed her until she was breathless.

"Got the message," Marilyn assured him as he drew his lips away from hers. Then she reached out and kissed him once more, just to be sure that she had gotten the message.

Give up seeing Marilyn? Hunter asked himself as he drove away from her small house. He would rather give up his right arm, or maybe a tooth or two. Sighing, he drove to the old rambling parsonage quickly, although he dreaded going into that huge house alone. *I'm tired of being lonely,* Hunter thought as he removed his tie and shirt, then shed the rest of his clothes and headed for the shower. He stood under the water for a long time as he thought about the lovely woman he had just left behind. *I'll do it!* he decided as he turned off the shower and toweled himself dry in the steamy bathroom. Reaching out, he wiped a clear spot on the mirror and looked at his naked body, studying the lean, muscled form critically. Not too bad for nearly forty, he decided, but he would try to get rid of that little roll on his waist. He left the bathroom and jumped into the chilly bed, burying himself under the covers. *Yes, I'll do it,* he told himself, looking wistfully at the empty half of the bed next to him.

He's coming to break it off, Marilyn thought sadly as she pulled on a pair of jeans and a shirt. It was late, but Hunter had just called. He had explained that he had just gotten back into town after several days in Houston, and he had asked if he could come over and talk to her about something important. Marilyn did not want to meet him in a flannel gown and a robe, so she dressed and ran a brush through her damp hair but skipped her makeup, feeling that it was not worth putting on her face to be told goodbye. *I guess he just didn't want to tell me over the phone,* she thought as she hung up her Sam Brown and folded the newspaper she had been reading. *He's decided to think of his career after all.* Marilyn's eyes filled with tears, but she dashed them away quickly and promised herself that she would shed no more until after he had gone. How on earth was she going to get used to life without Hunter? In the last three months she had fallen in love with him, and he had become the center of her barren existence. She knew he didn't love her, but she loved him, and for the time being that had been enough.

Hunter rang the doorbell and Marilyn let him in, motioning him to the couch. She sat across from him in a wing chair rather than in her usual place beside him. "What did you want to talk to me about?" she asked quietly, hoping that her inner trembling did not show. Although she hated it that he was breaking it off with her, she didn't want to make it hard on him, since he was doing only what he had to do.

Hunter looked distinctly uncomfortable. "Well," he began, "I've been doing a lot of thinking for the last few days, ever since our last date."

"The night I told you about the gossip," Marilyn said flatly.

"Yes, the night you told me that," Hunter continued. *Here it comes,* Marilyn thought. *He can't see me anymore.*

"Well, Marilyn, I wondered if you would do me the honor of becoming my wife."

"*What?*" Marilyn yelped, coming straight off the chair.

Hunter blushed a fiery shade of red. "I asked you to marry me," he repeated.

"You mean you didn't come over here to break it off?" Marilyn asked incredulously.

Hunter stood and opened the living room drapes, then took Marilyn in his arms. "W-what are you doing?" she stammered.

"I'm making it easy for Doris," he replied as he held Marilyn by the shoulders and kissed her until she was moaning. "I told you the other night that I wasn't going to stop seeing you and I meant it. Furthermore, I would like to marry you." The laughter in his eyes faded and he looked at her tenderly. "What do you say, Marilyn?" he asked softly.

Marilyn pulled the drapes and sat down in her customary place on the couch. "Don't you think you're going a little too far to quell the gossip?" she asked dryly.

The tender look on Hunter's face faded. "You honestly think I would go so far as to marry you just to shut this town up?" he demanded imperiously. "You must think I'm a real louse."

"I don't think that!" Marilyn defended herself vigorously. "But Hunter, your ministry means a lot to you and you were really upset the other night. What else am I supposed to think?"

"Well, I'm sure not asking you to marry me just to stop the gossip," Hunter replied firmly.

"Then why are you asking me?" Marilyn asked in a

small voice, hoping against hope that Hunter would say that he had fallen in love with her.

"Well, Marilyn, I'm lonely." Hunter stood up from the couch and thrust his hands into his pockets. He walked slowly from one end of the small living room to the other. "For years my relationship with God and my congregation have been enough, but it isn't anymore. I drive up to that big old parsonage and I can hardly stand to go inside because of the emptiness I know I'm going to find in there."

"I know the feeling," Marilyn murmured, thinking of the many times in the last eighteen months she had felt that way about her own house.

"And you have to admit that we're very physically attracted to each other," Hunter pointed out as Marilyn blushed. "Hey, now don't get embarrassed. That's an important part of life, too, you know, and I think with you and me it could be a very nice part of our lives together. And I just think we'd have a good life together. If the way you reached out to Suzanne and Jack Bohannon the other night is any indication, you have a loving and caring spirit that would make you a marvelous minister's wife, and I honestly think I could be a good husband to you."

"What about my divorce?" Marilyn asked quietly. "Will it hurt your career to marry a divorced woman?"

"I doubt it," Hunter replied. "Especially considering the circumstances of your divorce and the fact that you didn't initiate it."

Marilyn bit her lip. Although Hunter's reasoning was sound, he had not said the three magic words that she longed to hear. She had to know whether he loved her before she would commit herself. "What about love?" she asked. "We haven't talked about that."

Hunter stopped pacing the floor and sat down beside her. "There are many kinds of love, Marilyn, not just romantic love. For centuries marriages were arranged by the participants' parents, and most of those marriages lasted much better than those romantic liaisons that are made today." Marilyn winced, thinking of her own marriage. "I'm willing to bet that most of those couples grew to love each other sooner or later. And we do have love between us, Marilyn, even though it's not the kind of love that you're associating with marriage."

Marilyn nodded her head, thinking about what Hunter had said. So he didn't love her, at least not in a romantic sense. What had he said—that there were many kinds of love? He was talking about Christian love, of course. But would that be so bad? She'd had the other kind, and look how that had turned out. *And you do love him,* she thought. *You were just crushed when you thought he was coming over here to break it off. Even if he doesn't love you in a romantic way, he would always be good to you, and he would not leave you like Robert did. You at least could love him for the rest of your life.*

Marilyn reached out her hand and placed it into Hunter's. "If you're sure that you want to marry me, I would be delighted to become your wife," she said simply.

A joyous smile lit Hunter's face, and he reached out and pulled her to him, kissing her with all the joy that he could put into his caress. Marilyn responded instantly, pouring her love for Hunter into her kiss. She pulled him closer to her, running her fingers eagerly around his neck and into the hair at his nape, then lowering her hands until they had locked around his waist, hungrily exploring the appealing man who was soon to be her husband.

Hunter melted into her, delighting in the feel of her questing fingers on his virile body, straining to get closer to her. His hands involuntarily went to her shirt and he undid the top buttons, slipping his hand inside and finding one nipple. Marilyn strained toward his fingers, then gasped with pleasure as Hunter pushed away the fabric and bent his lips to her breast, touching her rosy nipple through the lacy bra with his tongue. His nimble fingers undid the front closure of her bra and he nosed it aside, finding her rosy peak with his tongue and running its velvet surface across it, eliciting an excited whimper from Marilyn as his intimate touch set her senses on fire. He feasted at her breast for long moments, then regretfully pulled her bra together and hooked it with trembling fingers, the glaze of passion in his eyes. "I better stop this before we jump the gun," he whispered as Marilyn buttoned the front of her shirt. Hunter reached down into his pocket and drew out a small box. "It was my mother's," he said, handing the box to her.

With trembling fingers Marilyn opened the box and withdrew a diamond solitaire set in platinum filigree. Hunter took the ring from her and placed it on her finger. "It's a perfect fit," she marveled.

"I cheated," Hunter admitted. "I called your mother and got your size."

"What did Mother say?" Marilyn asked hesitantly.

"She was so happy she cried," Hunter admitted as he picked her hand up and kissed it. *And I think I'm about to join her,* Marilyn thought as tears of joy stung her own eyes and she raised her lips to meet Hunter's once more.

She kissed him lingeringly and passionately, then withdrew herself from Hunter's embrace and headed toward the telephone, punching in a familiar number. "Doris? It's Marilyn. I promised you that you would be the first to know. Yes, we're getting married. No, I'm not sure when. Yes, I'll tell him. 'Bye."

Marilyn put down the receiver gently as Hunter whooped with laughter. "It'll be all over town by morning," he said as he wiped tears from his eyes. "I bet she could hardly wait to hang up."

"Well, I did promise her," Marilyn said lamely as Hunter took her in his arms once more.

Marilyn and Hunter set a wedding date for late February, and Marilyn began to plan her wedding in earnest. Because it was her second marriage, she and Hunter agreed to keep it small, and they planned on having just their families and their very closest friends at a small afternoon ceremony. Hunter suggested that they marry in the church, but Marilyn shied away from taking her vows in the same church where she had been married before, so they settled on the large parlor in the parsonage.

Marilyn and Tess arranged a day off together and drove into San Antonio to buy their dresses. It took them three exclusive shops, but they finally settled on a simple green taffeta for Tess and an exquisite taffeta in peach for Marilyn that gave her olive complexion a warm glow. Hunter's brother agreed to fly in all the way from Boston to be the best man, and a friend from Hunter's seminary days agreed to perform the ceremony. Marilyn ordered a cake from the bakery and arranged for a few photographs to be taken after the ceremony. She and Hunter picked out matching rings from one of the local jewelers, a simple design that she could wear with her diamond ring, and Marilyn made one other appointment that she considered essential to keep before she took her vows.

Marilyn drove up to Dr. Cooke's office and parked her truck, then she went inside and rang the little bell that was beside the receptionist's window. Almost instantly Mrs. Baxter, Dr. Cooke's nurse, appeared in the window. "It will be a few minutes, Marilyn," she said warmly as she smiled. "And congratulations on your upcoming marriage. Everyone in town is delighted for the two of you."

Delighted or just relieved? Marilyn asked herself cynically as she sat down in the waiting room and twisted the strap of her purse nervously. The announcement of their marriage had released another spate of gossip, but according to Tess, most of it had been friendly. So that problem is solved, Marilyn thought gratefully as Mrs. Baxter finally called her into the inner sanctum.

Dr. Cooke greeted her warmly and also congratulated her on her upcoming marriage. "I'm delighted that you're marrying again," he said frankly. "You deserve a little happiness."

"Thank you," Marilyn replied.

"I assume you're here for a premarital exam," Dr. Cooke added as he flipped through her chart.

"That and I want to go back on the pill," Marilyn blurted out.

Dr. Cooke looked surprised. "I would have thought you would want to have another child," he said slowly. Although it wasn't any of Dr. Cooke's business and he knew it, he felt that he had known Marilyn long enough to give him a right to speak out.

"I don't think so," Marilyn said softly. "At least not now. Hunter's never mentioned children, and we both know how upset Robert was when I got pregnant the way I did before."

Dr. Cooke shrugged. "I'll prescribe them, but if I were you, I'd discuss this with your fiancé before starting them. He may very well want to start a family very soon, considering the fact that neither of you is getting any younger, the minister in particular."

Marilyn nodded and Dr. Cooke left her to undress for the examination. She left the office thirty minutes later clutching a written prescription for her old brand of pills, the ones she used after Bobby was born. She would start the pills very soon, and she would not discuss this decision with Hunter. Although she had let down her guard enough to risk marrying him, there was no way she was going to expose herself to the kind of hurt she had known the night that Bobby died. There was no way on earth that she was going to have another child.

CHAPTER EIGHT

Marilyn peered into the mirror and brushed her hair nervously, then she carefully arranged the small clusters of rosebuds and baby's breath in her hair. She carefully made up her eyes and spread blusher on her cheeks with trembling fingers and painted her mouth with a soft peach lip gloss to match her dress. "Do I look all right?" she asked anxiously as Tess bustled into the huge old bedroom.

"You look fine," Tess reassured her warmly. "In fact, you look just beautiful." She sat down on the bed and looked around the room. "Did you say that this is the master bedroom?" she asked casually, peering around at the old but lovely oak pieces and the huge brass bed.

Marilyn nodded. "Hunter let me use it this afternoon," she confirmed as she dusted her nose with translucent powder. "I moved most of my things over here yesterday." She gestured to the antique wardrobe next to the bed where she had hung her winter clothes. "My renters move in next week."

"You're going to keep the house?" Tess asked incredulously. "I would have thought you would have wanted to get rid—er, sell it."

Marilyn shrugged. "It isn't the fault of the house that I was so unhappy there. And if you want the truth, we could use the rental income. I'll be making a little profit on the rent." She stepped into her bone sandals and turned around slowly for Tess. "Are you sure I look all right?" she asked again.

"Yes, Marilyn, you look beautiful," Tess assured her.

The door opened and Marilyn's lively little mother fluttered into the room. "Are you ready, dear?" she asked, her eyes twinkling. "Hunter's down there pacing like a caged tiger. He's so nervous, it's funny."

"I guess it's because he's never been married before," Marilyn said as she smoothed an imaginary wrinkle in her dress. That would certainly be the only reason that Hunter would be nervous.

"Then what's your excuse?" Tess teased as Marilyn blushed.

Maggie White reached out and handed Marilyn a wrapped package. "Hunter said this is your wedding present," she said. "He thought you might want to wear it for the ceremony."

Marilyn took the package and unwrapped it with trembling fingers. Cooing softly, she carefully lifted a small diamond necklace from the box and held it up unbelievingly. "Isn't it beautiful!" she said as she tried to put it on with fingers that wouldn't quite work. Tess brushed aside Marilyn's ineffective hands and hooked the necklace latch herself. The diamond, not too big or too little, sparkled warmly from the choker-length chain. "He didn't have to do that," she said softly, touched because Robert had never given her anything nice like this.

"A man in love does all kind of things he doesn't have to do," Maggie said gently. Marilyn winced inwardly, knowing that Hunter did not love her, or at least did not love her in that way, but in a way that made his gift just that much more generous.

Maggie handed Marilyn a small bouquet of roses as her tall father appeared at the door. "Everyone's ready," he reported softly as he reached out and hugged Marilyn to him. "Oh, girl, I hope you're happy, I really do," he said with a father's love.

"I will be, Daddy," Marilyn assured him with conviction.

Maggie went on down the stairs into the large parlor.

On Tess's signal, Susan Thomas started playing the Wedding March on the piano and Tess descended the stairs, followed by Marilyn and her father. Her eyes lowered in shyness, Marilyn did not look up until she was almost beside Hunter and the minister, then when she did look up she saw such an expression of tenderness on Hunter's face that she almost gasped. If he had not told her differently, she would have sworn at that moment that he loved her.

The minister, an old friend of Hunter's, performed a simple, moving ceremony. He read the passages from Corinthians on love, and said that between two Christians this kind of love is the ideal to be reached for. At Marilyn's request, he read the passages from Proverbs describing a responsible husband and a virtuous wife. Then Hunter and Marilyn spoke their vows clearly and firmly, and as Marilyn looked into Hunter's eyes and vowed "until death do us part," she knew at that moment that she would be with this man until death separated them. She loved him, and although maybe he didn't love her in the way that she wanted to be loved, he would never leave her.

The minister pronounced them husband and wife and Hunter reached out and took her in his arms, kissing her firmly but passionately and stealing the breath from her momentarily. They were greeted with a rush of congratulations and Marilyn finally was able to meet Hunter's brother, a wealthy attorney from Boston. Sam Templeton was a little older than Hunter, but he had the same piercing black eyes and compassionate spirit, and Marilyn wondered briefly how he had ever made it in the cutthroat world of corporate law. He openly expressed his delight that Hunter had finally married such a lovely woman and wished them both many years together. Maggie and Tess were both sniffing back tears of joy, seeing this marriage as a sign that Marilyn had finally put her deep grief behind her and that she was ready for a full life again.

The photographer ordered them around for a few minutes, taking various group photos, then they visited with their guests for a few minutes before cutting the cake. They were in no hurry to leave this afternoon, since they had agreed earlier to spend a quiet weekend at a cabin in the country in deference to their limited budget. They cut their cake and obediently fed each other a piece, the photographer snapping away merrily, then they and their guests enjoyed cake and punch and finger sandwiches.

At Marilyn's mother's bidding, they opened some of their gifts and oohed and aahed over both their practical gifts of cookware and linens and the delicate pieces of silver hollowware that a few of the wealthier of the congregation had sent. Marilyn was just opening the last of the presents when the doorbell rang and someone, Marilyn was not sure who, answered the bell and called Hunter to the door. He came back a few minutes later with a strange look on his face and whispered to her that she needed to hurry. *Hurry?* Marilyn thought. *I thought we agreed we didn't have to hurry.* Nevertheless, she obediently hurried with the last package and then Hunter hustled her up the stairs, pushing her gently into the big bedroom where she had dressed earlier.

She had removed her dress and her slip and was standing there in her bra and panties when Hunter burst in, carrying both their suitcases. He stopped for a moment, staring with naked longing at her scantily clad form, then quickly whipped off his coat, shirt, and pants, tossing them on the bed. "You're going to have to repack," he said as he unselfconsciously started rummaging around in his drawers, unmindful of the effect his near nudity was having on Marilyn's pulse rate. "Our honeymoon plans have been changed."

"What?" Marilyn asked absently, tearing her eyes away from Hunter's broad chest.

"Our honeymoon," Hunter said as he dumped the contents of his suitcase on the bed and started filling it with items from his drawers. "You need to get rid of all your winter stuff and pack some resort clothes. And you need to hurry. Our plane leaves out of San Antonio in two and a half hours."

Slowly coming out of her stupor, Marilyn snapped open her suitcase. "What plane? What kind of resort clothes? Where are we going?" She carefully removed her jeans and shirts, then pawed through the drawers she had appropriated yesterday and found her summer shorts and blouses and packed them. "What else do I need?" she asked, finding and packing her two swimsuits. "And would you kindly tell me where we're going?" she demanded.

"You need a couple of evening outfits," Hunter suggested. "Something summery and romantic."

"I don't have anything like that!" Marilyn wailed. "And will you please tell me where we're going?"

"Don't worry about the dresses then," Hunter replied as he hauled out his swimsuits and packed several summer shirts and slacks, then piled in some jeans and knit tops. "We'll buy them down there."

Marilyn swiftly crossed the room and took Hunter by the shoulders, staring into his face impatiently. "Hunter Templeton, will you please tell me where we are going?"

Taking advantage of the situation, Hunter slid both of his arms around Marilyn's waist, hauling her closer to him. Before she could protest, he had lowered his lips to hers and was kissing her thoroughly, his lips claiming hers with passionate possession. He ran one of his hands down Marilyn's back and over her bottom, pressing her closer to his hard, warm body, making her aware of his need for her. Forgetting her impatience, Marilyn pressed herself closer to him, her body enflamed by his closeness. The hair on his chest tickled her breasts through the lacy bra she wore, and the hard muscles in Hunter's legs throbbed against her. Forgetting the rush, Hunter reached up and unhooked Marilyn's bra, letting it fall to the floor as he first tasted one breast then the other with deep hunger. "I've wanted for so long to have the right to do that," he murmured as Marilyn arched toward his questing mouth, eager to feel more of Hunter's tender lips on the sensitive peaks. Hunter let his lips travel slowly up her shoulders and her neck, leaving a path of goose pimples where his touch had been. "We have to get ready," he said as he kissed her once more and pushed her away from him. "We can make love all night once we get to Cancún."

"Cancún?" Marilyn cried as she picked up her bra and put it back on, the passionate glaze in her eyes fading to an astonished stare. "How are we going to pay for that?"

"We're not," Hunter admitted as he pulled on a pair of lightweight slacks. "Here, this will be good for the plane ride," he told her as he opened the wardrobe and handed her a simple cotton dress with a matching jacket. "Your necklace just about cleaned me out. Oh, could you please hurry?"

"I'm not the one who started necking," Marilyn snapped as she pulled on a slip and the dress. She freshened her makeup, took the flowers out of her hair, brushed it, and picked up her purse. "So who's sending us on this honeymoon? Your brother?" she asked, thinking of Sam Templeton's generous spirit.

"No, although I wouldn't have been surprised if he had offered. No, the airplane and hotel reservations were made and paid for by James McBride."

"*James McBride?*" Marilyn stood speechless for long moments. "You have to be putting me on."

"Yeah, I know," Hunter said as he snapped shut the last

suitcase and picked them both up. Marilyn followed with Hunter's duffel bag and her makeup kit. "You could have knocked me over with a feather when he rang the doorbell. He also handed me a very generous stack of traveler's checks for spending money."

"I can't believe it," Marilyn said as she followed him down the stairs. "I simply can't believe it. Why, the old coot has a heart after all!"

Marilyn peered down at the swirling waters of the Caribbean, strangely dark in the purple dusk. Excitement and nervousness curled in her stomach as she realized that she was really married to Hunter now, and that in just a few hours they would be in the privacy of their hotel room, holding each other and becoming one in the flesh. Ever since they had kissed and caressed each other so intimately in Hunter's bedroom this afternoon, she had been very aware that tonight they would be making love in the fullest sense of the word, and although the thought thrilled Marilyn, to some extent it also frightened her. It was one thing to cling to Hunter with abandon when she knew that they would be calling a halt before any real intimacy was achieved. But tonight there would be no stopping. They would be carrying their kisses and embraces to their natural conclusion, and that knowledge made Marilyn nervous. She toyed with the rest of her airline meal and scanned again the travel brochure Hunter had picked up in the San Antonio airport.

"Cancún sounds really nice," Marilyn said as Hunter peered over her shoulder at the brochure. "This says that it's only been there ten years or so, but that there's lots of beaches and jungle to explore, plus a certain amount of nightlife. Do you like to go out at night?" she asked, suddenly aware of how little she really knew of the man she had just married.

"Some," Hunter nodded. "But frankly, I can think of a much more pleasurable way to spend my nights on my honeymoon," he said softly as Marilyn blushed prettily, her nervousness increasing at Hunter's provocative words.

The flight attendant took their trays and told everyone to fasten their seat belts, then the airplane made a smooth landing. Hunter took Marilyn's hand as the warm blast of air hit them at the door of the plane. "Oh, isn't this lovely," Marilyn said as she breathed in the warm, tangy air flavored by the salt of the sea and the lush tropical flowers of the region.

"Lovely," Hunter confirmed as they strode toward the terminal.

They retrieved their luggage and got in the hotel limousine that was to take them into Cancún, a few miles down the road. Darkness had fallen and Marilyn was not able to see much, but soon they were driving through Cancún. They drove out over a causeway and before too long the limousine had pulled up in front of a huge luxury hotel only yards from the beach.

"Can you believe this?" Hunter breathed.

"Not quite," Marilyn admitted as they stepped out of the limousine.

They climbed the wide steps and strode slowly into the luxury hotel, resplendent with natural wood decor and lush tropical paintings and artwork. The room clerk was slow but friendly, and before too long they were going up the elevator to their suite of rooms on the tenth floor. They unlocked the door and stared with mingled surprise and pleasure at the small sitting room decorated with plush furnishings in a lush tropical color scheme, and the spacious bedroom that was dominated by a huge bed.

Hunter closed the door slowly behind him and slipped his arm around Marilyn. "Let's look around a little," he said softly. Marilyn wandered into the bedroom and tested the bed, then peeked into the bathroom and was astounded to find a huge sunken tub. She was just coming out of the bathroom when Hunter called to her. "Come here, Marilyn. I want you to see this."

Marilyn followed the sound of Hunter's voice out to the balcony off the sitting room, and she gasped at the sight of the majestic Caribbean bathed in moonlight, pounding the curving shore. The lights of the other hotels twinkled down the beach but were unable to obscure the scattering of stars that could compete with the brightness of the moon.

"Oh, Hunter, it's beautiful," she murmured as he took her into his arms. She melted into him willingly and kissed him lovingly, but as she remembered that tonight was to be their wedding night she stiffened involuntarily, nervousness diluting the passion she had felt just hours ago.

Hunter released her, a puzzled frown on his face, and answered a knock at the door. The smiling bellboy brought in their bags and graciously accepted his tip, then Hunter and Marilyn were once more alone. He looked searchingly at her face, noting the anxiety she could not quite hide, and bit his lip. Bridal nerves? But she had been married before, hadn't she?

Marilyn kicked off her shoes and sat in one of the plush chairs of the sitting room. Hunter was going to be making love to her very soon now. Was she ready? Oh, she wished that they had made love this afternoon in his big bedroom in the parsonage. She hadn't been nervous then, and would have responded unselfconsciously to Hunter's embrace. But she was nervous now. Nervous? She was just plain scared. She schooled her face to what she hoped was calm pleasantness and smiled at Hunter. "Are you ready for bed?" she asked in a voice that only trembled a little.

Hunter shook his head and sat down beside her. "I'm hungry," he admitted. "Let's order some sandwiches from room service, and while they're bringing them I want you to tell me why you're so nervous you're about to jump off that couch."

Marilyn stared with astonishment as he got up and went to the telephone and ordered a plate of roast beef sandwiches, then returned to her and sat down beside her, taking her trembling hand in his. "Is it bridal nerves?" he asked tenderly.

"Well, sort of," Marilyn admitted as she lightly stroked his callused hand with her soft fingers. She bit her lip and tried to find the right words to explain her feelings to Hunter. "I've never been with anyone else but Robert, and frankly it wasn't very good for us. I didn't know what to do, and I don't think he did either. And then later, of course, it was as sour as the rest of our marriage." She got up and paced the room, her face scarlet. "I mean, you're a minister, you've lived by the rules of the church . . ." She trailed off and looked at him miserably. "Do you know what to do?" she asked finally.

Hunter sat back and looked at Marilyn, laughing and blushing as brightly as she had. "So we're a fine pair—a scared bride and a crusty old bachelor bridegroom. Come here, Marilyn," he said tenderly, patting the seat beside him. Marilyn sat down beside him and he took her hand in his. "You know, in my years of counseling, I've often observed that the sexual relationship that a couple has is only as good as the rest of the relationship. If the marriage is happy, the sex is good. Sure, you and Robert were inexperienced, but if your marriage had been good, that inexperience would have gone by the wayside fast."

Hunter stroked Marilyn's arm gently, his fingers trembling. "Now, I spent five years in the navy, so I'm not a total greenhorn. But I'll admit to you that I haven't made love to a woman in many years, because when I went into the seminary I vowed that I would never preach one standard while I practiced another. And it isn't because I haven't wanted to either! So I'm a little nervous, too, Marilyn, but I promise that I'll make it just as good for you as I know how to. Is that all right?"

"Of course that's all right," Marilyn said softly, her heart full of love for this big gentle man who didn't mind admitting that he was nervous too. At that moment a knock on the door announced the arrival of their sandwiches and, her nervousness fading, Marilyn devoured two of the thick, spicy delights.

Marilyn stood before the mirror and brushed her damp hair, the white chiffon nightgown clinging to her slender curves under the billowing robe. She and Hunter had eaten their sandwiches and sat talking for a while, their nervousness fading and their excitement building to a high pitch. Finally Hunter had excused himself and had gone into the bathroom, emerging a few minutes later wearing a blue velour robe with a hood thrown over his damp hair. Marilyn had taken her gown and robe, purchased during her shopping trip with Tess, into the bathroom with her and had showered quickly, rubbing herself dry and squirting on a little of her favorite perfume before she donned her nightgown and robe. Would Hunter be pleased with her tonight? she wondered as she turned out the light and left the bathroom.

Her husband had turned back the bed in her absence and was sitting on the side, absently flipping through a stack of brochures he had picked up in the lobby.

"What do you want to do tomorrow?" she asked as she sat down beside him and slid her arm around his waist.

Hunter smiled and shrugged. "Let's decide that tomorrow," he said as he tossed the brochures on the table beside the bed. "Let's not commit ourselves. We may want to sleep late." He reached over and turned off the overhead light, leaving one small hurricane lamp burning beside the bed. "I want to see you when I make love to you," he explained softly as he stood up, drawing Marilyn up as he gently reached out and untied the belt of her robe, pushing it off her shoulders and letting the frothy confection fall to the floor. "I've dreamed for months of having the freedom to do this," he murmured as he reached out and kissed Marilyn's bare shoulder tenderly. Marilyn reached out and kissed his face gently, her fingers touching the red hair of his sideburns.

"I've wanted to touch you too," she admitted shyly. "I was even embarrassed at first, feeling that way about a minister."

"Oh, Marilyn," Hunter said, cupping her face tenderly in his big hands, "Ministers need to be loved too." He leaned forward and kissed her tenderly. "Some of the most beautiful love poetry in the world was written by a man of God. Have you ever heard it?" he asked.

"I don't know," Marilyn admitted.

Hunter kissed her lips softly as he started to speak.

> Rise up, my love, my fair one, and come away.
> For, lo the winter is past, the rain is over and gone;
> The flowers appear on the earth; the time of the singing of birds is come,
> and the voice of the turtle is heard in our land.

Marilyn nodded, her eyes stinging at the beauty of the beloved old scriptures. " 'I am my beloved's, and his desire is for me,' " she quoted softly. "Oh, Hunter, make love to me. I'm not afraid anymore. I just want you!"

"Oh, I'm going to," Hunter replied as he reached up and pushed down the straps that were holding her gown in place, then smoothed the silky fabric down to her waist, exposing her firm, high breasts to his smoldering gaze.

He bent his head and took one rosy nipple into his mouth, teasing it with his lips until it was a hard knot. He bathed the other breast in the softness of his lips, then gently pushed her gown down her hips. He gently touched her soft stomach as the gown fell into a heap on the floor. "Marilyn, you are so incredibly beautiful that there are no real words to describe you."

Boldly, warmed by his caressing words and touch, Marilyn untied the belt of his robe and pushed it from his shoulders. She gazed for the first time at Hunter's unclad body, seeing the strength in his tall, muscled form. His shoulders were straight and broad, his strong chest and long legs covered with soft reddish hair that would be heaven to touch, his lean hips strong and inviting. Marilyn stepped away from her discarded clothes and put her arms around Hunter, lifting her face for his kiss.

Hunter kissed her slowly, and then in an instant he had scooped her up and placed her tenderly on the bed, lying down beside her and kissing her neck and her throat. He touched her gently, lest her former nervousness return, kissing and caressing her neck and her breasts, setting her slowly aflame with his sensuous touch. As Marilyn moaned in pleasure beneath his tender ministrations, his hand crept to her waist and hips, stroking and touching her as her desire flared. She wiggled her breasts closer to Hunter's loving touch, feeling shooting spasms of delight curl through her stomach and even lower. *Oh, sweet sweet love,* she thought as Hunter's lips tormented one nipple until Marilyn thought she would faint with pleasure. "Oh, Hunter, that feels so wonderful," she whispered as he tormented her waist with his fingers.

"I know," he whispered. "Would you like to touch me now?" he asked.

"Yes, my darling, oh, yes," Marilyn replied as she reached out and caressed Hunter's broad chest with her fingers. Wanting to give Hunter the same kind of pleasure he was giving her, Marilyn ran her hands down his sides and around his flat waist, feeling the trembling of his hard body at the intimacy of her touch. "Roll over," she said softly. "I can't touch you like this."

Hunter rolled over on his back and gave Marilyn the freedom to explore his body thoroughly, satisfying her own curiosity about his secrets as she built his excitement to an almost unbearable pitch. "Do you like this?" she would ask as she touched him in some new, intimate place. "Or this?" she would ask as her lips caressed him tenderly. By the time that Hunter finally sat up and pushed her gently back to the bed, there wasn't an inch of his enticing body that she did not know with the same intimacy with which she knew her own.

"My turn," Hunter said as he tenderly pushed Marilyn over on her back. His lips explored Marilyn's body as her lips had explored his, seeking out every pleasure point and tormenting it thoroughly with his lips and his tongue. "Do you like this?" he asked as he suckled first one breast, then the other. "Does this feel good?" he would ask as he touched her in some new, intimate way, feeling rather than hearing Marilyn's passionate affirmation of the delight of his touch. *Is this pleasure what it's all about?* Marilyn wondered as Hunter's lips made a delicate foray from her breasts to her navel. *Is this really possible?* she wondered as Hunter's hands wandered even lower, exciting her body with their intimate, knowing touch. Finally, as Marilyn thought that she couldn't possibly stand any more pleasure, Hunter parted her legs gently, and with an erotic tenderness that took Marilyn's breath away, he claimed her as his own.

Sensations that Marilyn did not even know possible flooded her. Shivers of delight coursed through her as their intimately entwined bodies moved together in a ritual as old as time. Where Hunter led, she willingly followed, held in thrall by the delight that they shared. She gasped as the pressure mounted inside her, a pressure that she had never felt before and that she did not understand, but it was so incredibly sweet. Hunter moved passionately above her, filling her with such incredible sensations that it was all she could do not to cry out. When the pressure had become almost unbearable, something inside her burst. Lights flickered behind her closed lids and she cried out softly, murmuring Hunter's name sharply as the swirling mists threatened to claim her. She felt Hunter explode inside her, her name on his lips, then they collapsed in a damp tangle of arms and legs.

They lay still for long minutes, then Hunter moved off her and pulled her close to his side. "I don't think we had too much trouble with that, did we?" he asked softly as he caressed the soft skin of Marilyn's stomach.

Marilyn raised bemused eyes to meet his. "I never realized it could be so wonderful," she whispered. "That was so beautiful."

"I could tell that it was something new for you," Hunter admitted as he explored her mouth gently with his own. "It was new for me too, Marilyn. I never felt that, even back in the old days."

"I'm glad," Marilyn said fiercely. "I'm glad I could give you that."

"Of course, I'm greedy," Hunter said wickedly as he pressed her into the tangled sheets and pressed his lips against hers. "I could do with some more."

"More?" Marilyn asked bemusedly. "Why, we just got through!"

"Got through?" Hunter snickered. "My dear wife, we're only getting started," he whispered as he bore her down into the sheets and covered her body with his own.

* * *

Marilyn and Hunter didn't even make it out of bed until almost noon the next day, enthralled as they were with each other and the passionate bond that they were busy forging. Still lethargic from their repeated bouts of lovemaking, they ventured no farther than the beach in front of the hotel, slathering themselves with suntan lotion and soaking up the hot tropical sun. Marilyn lay still for a while, watching the tourists through lowered lids, then she sat up and started sifting the warm white sand between her fingers. Before she could stop herself, she found herself fashioning the damp sand into a small castle.

"What are you doing?" Hunter asked as he watched Marilyn mold the sand expertly between her fingers.

"Building a castle, of course," Marilyn replied as she expertly piled and patted the sand into the main body of the castle. She built one tower carefully, groaning when the too-dry sand started to crumble.

"You mean we get to come to this fancy Caribbean resort and hobnob with all the wealthies, and you're going to build a sand castle?" Hunter teased her lightly.

"Of course," Marilyn replied calmly. "My sister and I used to build the best ones on the coast."

Hunter sat up and watched her carefully. "Well, I guess I can contribute to this effort," he said as he sat up and started to mold the sand. Between them, in about a half hour they had fashioned a superb castle, complete with a moat and turrets. Hunter was so impressed that he insisted on taking a picture of the castle. "Our first sand castle," he teased Marilyn proudly. "We can show our kids these pictures someday."

Marilyn froze, mumbling what she hoped was a suitable reply. *Surely he didn't mean it,* she told herself as she watched the waves pound the shore, *because I have no intention of ever having another child to love and lose.*

Hunter and Marilyn spent a lovely week in Cancún.

They rose late after making love into the wee hours of the night and spent their days swimming, sight-seeing, and shopping. One day they smeared on insect repellent and went on a guided tour into the lush tropical jungle that ended up at the Mayan ruins of El Rey. Hunter was impressed with the antiquity of the ruins of the ancient trade center, but Marilyn was more taken with the lush vegetation of the jungle that sported a profusion of brightly colored native flowers. Another day they went shopping in the market, oohing and aahing over the native articles such as hammocks that were made of henequen, and Hunter bought Marilyn three of the ridiculously low-priced embroidered cotton dresses, also made locally.

One afternoon they rented a boat and a driver, and Marilyn taught Hunter to water-ski, laughing teasingly at his numerous spills. In the evenings they dined at all the fancy restaurants, sampling the local delicacies such as *mucbil pollo,* a chicken tamale pie, and all the fresh seafood dishes. They saw a couple of floor shows in the hotels, but usually found that they were much more eager to go back to their hotel room after a walk on the beach and explore each other's bodies passionately, joining together in sensual abandon.

"You know, I hate to go home," Marilyn admitted as she and Hunter strolled down the beach on their last night in Cancún. "This week has been wonderful."

"Not scared of making love anymore, huh?" Hunter teased.

"It sounds silly now, doesn't it?" Marilyn said sheepishly.

"Not silly," Hunter replied tenderly. "Sweet, somehow." He took her hand and looked out over the water. "I was afraid that maybe I wouldn't measure up to your former husband," he admitted softly.

"Oh, Hunter, if you only knew," Marilyn whispered,

slipping her arms around his waist. "If you only knew the joy I've known with you this last week."

"Well, I'm glad," Hunter said fervently. "I know it's selfish, but I'm glad that I was the one to bring you that kind of pleasure."

"I'm glad too," Marilyn admitted, reaching up and linking her arms around Hunter's neck. "Want to do a little necking on the beach?" she invited wickedly.

Hunter reached down and captured her mouth with his own. Even after a week of tasting his kisses often, the touch of his lips on hers thrilled her. Marilyn melted into Hunter, basking in the sensual storm that his touch aroused in her. The breeze off the ocean ruffled their hair and blew her frothy skirt out from her body, bathing them both in a soft warm spray of mist from the ocean. Hunter ran his hands down Marilyn's sides, anchoring her in front of him so that she could not move away, as he kissed every inch of her salty face. "I have a better idea," he whispered. "Want to go back to the room and go all the way?" he asked as he leered at her teasingly.

"All the way it is!" Marilyn said as Hunter took her hand.

In spite of her high heels, they ran all the way back to the hotel, slowing down only a little as they sped through the lobby, and punching the elevator button three times in their impatience. Finally they were on their floor. Hunter fumbled with the key and dropped it in his haste, then accidentally stepped on Marilyn's fingers as she tried to retrieve it for him. "Oww!" she cried as she removed her sore fingers.

"Marilyn, I'm sorry," Hunter said as he knelt next to her and kissed her fingers.

"See where all that lust will get you?" Marilyn teased as she stood and inserted the key in the lock.

Hunter followed her into the room and shut the door

behind her. "This week has been more than lust, and you know it," he murmured as he drew her to him and kissed her hungrily.

"Yes, it has," Marilyn agreed as soon as Hunter released her lips.

He eagerly stripped off his shirt and slacks, then unzipped Marilyn's dress and pushed it off her shoulders. She pulled his T-shirt over his head, then he divested her of her slip and panty hose. She pushed Hunter onto the bed and pulled off his socks, leaving him clad in only his briefs. Deftly he unhooked her bra and tore it from her body, eagerly feasting on the sight and the taste of her rose-tipped breasts. Marilyn's nipples hardened in the anticipation of Hunter's sensual touch, bringing a smile to the lips that lightly grazed them.

Marilyn savored Hunter's touch as he explored her willing body, no longer having to ask what she liked him to do. With eager, experienced fingers Marilyn brought Hunter delight, touching all his vulnerable places and watching with sensual appreciation as Hunter blossomed under her touch. Daringly, she slid down his body and slowly removed his remaining garment, pitching it across the floor, then gasped as Hunter sat up and did the same to hers. "I can hardly wait to have you once more," he murmured as he drew her down on top of him.

"Are you absolutely sure that this isn't lust?" Marilyn teased as she nibbled the salty hair on Hunter's chest lightly.

"So what if it is?" Hunter taunted.

Wickedly she tormented him with her fingers and her mouth, exciting herself as much as she was exciting Hunter by her erotic touch. Lightly, coaxingly, she let her hands drift lower, teasing and tormenting Hunter sensuously until he was moaning. "Roll over," he instructed her softly.

Marilyn shook her head, her hair a dark, tousled cloud around her face. "I want to make love to you," she stated simply as she moved herself over Hunter and made them one, bringing a gasp of delight from her willing prisoner.

Hunter let her set the pace and take the lead this time, flowing with her, following her into her own sensual realm. Marilyn gloried in her power to please Hunter, to bring him joy, and she pleasured him in every way that she knew how, as the sensual pressure began to build in her own body. Knowing now what was going to happen to her, Marilyn held herself still a moment, then resumed her motions until Hunter was at the edge of the precipice. She took the plunge and they toppled off together, silently spinning around in a free fall through space. Exhausted, Marilyn collapsed against Hunter, her breathing slowly returning to normal.

"Still think it was lust?" Hunter asked quietly as Marilyn lay curled into the curve of his hip, staring out the window at the moon lighting up the sky.

"Of course not," Marilyn replied, shifting to bring her back closer to his chest. "We did pretty well for a scared bride and a crusty old bachelor bridegroom, didn't we?" she laughed softly.

"Not so scared and not so crusty anymore, are we?" Hunter said as he rubbed her arm absently.

Marilyn shook her head. "Wouldn't it be something if we managed to get you pregnant on our honeymoon?" he asked gently.

Marilyn forced herself not to stiffen in his arms. "Yes, that really would be something," she said softly as she thought of the pills in the bottom of her makeup case. "But it isn't very likely, I'm afraid."

"Oh, well, it will happen sooner or later," Hunter replied as he curled his arm around her and held her close.

His deep, even breathing soon told Marilyn that he was asleep.

Marilyn laid awake for a long time, staring out the window at the moonlight. *No, Hunter, it won't happen sooner or later,* she thought as she blinked back tears. *There's no way I'm going to let it happen.* She had risked enough by loving and marrying again, especially by marrying a man who didn't love her in return. *I'll have to talk to him when we get back,* she promised herself, *and tell him how I feel. It isn't fair to let him go on thinking there might be a child soon, when there isn't going to be one at all. Loving Hunter is risk enough. There is no way I'm going to risk loving and losing Hunter's child.* Promising herself to settle this with him when they got home, Marilyn closed her eyes and willed herself to go to sleep.

CHAPTER NINE

"Hunter, do you want to accept this invitation to Elder Wright's house for dinner next week?" Marilyn asked as she sifted through the mail and sipped her morning coffee.

Hunter reached over and took the invitation from her. "Sure, why not? They're super people, and we could use a night out."

"Yes, they are nice people," Marilyn said. "All right, I'll call them and accept." She took the invitation from Hunter and put it in the pile of mail that she would tend to later. "Will you be home in time for dinner?" she asked as she walked around the table with her empty coffee cup, stopping to kiss Hunter on the cheek as she passed by. *I love him more by the day,* she thought as her heart swelled with love and admiration for the man she married.

"I'm not sure, hon," Hunter replied as she poured him another cup of coffee. "I'm getting my sermon whipped into shape this morning, and I have three sick members in three different San Antonio hospitals to visit this afternoon, so I'm not sure when I'll be home."

Marilyn's face fell. "And I have to go on duty at seven," she replied. Her face brightened. "Tell you what. If you think it would be all right, you make those hospital visits this morning, we can spend the afternoon together, and I'll cook dinner before I have to go to work."

"Or better yet. We make the hospital visits together this morning, spend the afternoon together, and I'll write my sermon this evening. How's that?"

"Great," Marilyn smiled. She carried their plates to the sink and ran a tub full of water. "Oh, how I miss my dishwasher," she moaned mockingly as she plunged her hands into the hot soapy water. "Seriously, Hunter, do you mind if I keep working? I wouldn't give quitting my job a second thought. This job of yours seems to be a two-person responsibility." And it was. Between two church services on Sunday, visitation, Sunday school, the prison ministry, counseling troubled members, and sermon preparation, Hunter hardly had time to breathe, and Marilyn found that she could really ease his burden in several areas. If she were available all the time, she could make a real difference.

"If you care to look at last month's budget, you wouldn't even ask," Hunter replied frankly. "As long as you can stand the pace, I can sure use the financial help. But maybe you will be able to go back to the office someday after the children come," he said as he brought her his empty coffee cup. "Can you be ready to go in thirty minutes?" he asked as he wandered out of the big old kitchen.

Marilyn nodded as Hunter left the room. *I've got to talk to him,* she thought as she scrubbed the congealed egg off a plate. *But there never seems to be any time.* Ever since they had returned from their week in Cancún a month ago, they had both been kept so busy with the joint responsibilities of his ministry and being his wife that they had hardly had time to say hello, much less conduct a serious discussion. *And then you don't really want to talk to him about it,* Marilyn chided herself as she rinsed the last of the cups. *You don't want to tell Hunter that you don't want any more children.* Admitting to herself that she was the coward that Hunter once accused her of being, she scrubbed out the skillet and rinsed it, trying desperately to think of some way that she could break the news to Hunter gently. This morning was the first time since their honeymoon that he had mentioned children, and she had been hoping that he had forgotten about it.

Marilyn dressed in a simple skirt and blouse and made

up her face, ready a full five minutes before Hunter had specified. She found him in his study, a pair of reading glasses perched on his nose, going over next Sunday's sermon file. "What you gonna hit 'em with this week?" she asked teasingly.

"The sin of pride," Hunter said, laying his notes aside and pulling her down onto his lap, kissing her thoroughly.

"I notice you still haven't preached on lust," Marilyn teased, laughing when Hunter blushed.

"I couldn't preach it without turning three shades of red and dropping my notes," Hunter admitted, pushing Marilyn off his lap and walking with her to the door. "Here's the hospitals and the room numbers," he said as he shoved a piece of paper into her hand.

They had just locked the front door when the telephone started to ring. "Oh, let it ring," Marilyn said as Hunter fumbled with the keys.

"I can't. It might be something important," Hunter replied as he unlocked the front door and went in. He answered it on the fifth ring and listened for a moment, then slammed down the receiver and bolted for the front door. "It's Ryan Bohannon again," he said as he took her hand and they ran for the truck.

"Are we taking them in again?" Marilyn asked as she jumped into the truck.

"No, but we still need to get up there on the double to be with Jack and Suzanne. Ryan's grandmother said that they had just taken him in. It's bad this time, Marilyn, real bad."

The other hospital patients forgotten, Hunter drove to San Antonio as fast as he dared, breaking every speed law in the state. Marilyn stared out the window with unseeing eyes. *It never stops,* she thought sadly. *You think you're going to be happy for a while, but the sadness never goes away. Oh, Suzanne, you're going to be so lonely after he's gone,* she thought as tears glazed her eyes. She willed them away and by the time she and Hunter reached the hospital, she was ready to be the calm, supportive friend that Suzanne needed.

Suzanne and Jack were in the waiting room, eager for a doctor to appear and tell them something. Hunter went to the beverage machine and got four cups of coffee, and the four of them sat down together. "Have you heard anything since you brought him in?" Hunter asked quietly.

"Not a word," Jack said helplessly. "We haven't heard anything at all since we talked to that new surgeon last Friday."

"New surgeon?" Marilyn asked.

Suzanne turned tired eyes in Marilyn's direction. "Well, you know that the standard surgical techniques were useless in Ryan's case, but Dr. Gold has developed some new technique that he thinks might have been useful if Ryan hadn't been so very ill. The doctor told us to take Ryan home and try to get him a little stronger before he attempts to operate. That's what we were doing until this morning, when Ryan got sicker again. So we brought him in, and Dr. Gold is in there with him now."

"Oh, Suzanne, I hope—well, you know," Marilyn stammered, not wanting to put it into words.

"Well, Ryan's in the Lord's hands," Suzanne said quietly as Marilyn nodded.

The young, thin doctor came out of the examining room and walked over to where the four of them were sitting. He pulled up a chair and straddled it, his long legs sticking out in front of him. "Mr. and Mrs. Bohannon, I'll put it to you like this. If Ryan were not so sick and so weak, I'd give him an excellent prognosis and wheel him into surgery without blinking twice. But he's a very weak, very sick little boy, and I frankly doubt that he will survive the surgery. But if I don't try, he's going to die anyway. So I wanted to talk to you. We'll make this decision together."

Another no-answer situation, Marilyn thought as she looked over at Hunter, who was in turn whispering with Jack. Jack nodded and turned to the doctor. "Our minister is here with us, and we'd like a moment of prayer before we make a decision like that."

Dr. Gold nodded. "Yes, we all could use God's guidance today," he said as he watched them bow their heads. As she shut her eyes, Marilyn whispered a silent prayer.

After the brief silence, Jack Bohannon said, "Amen" and raised his head. "Go ahead with the surgery," he said softly.

The doctor scurried away, and Jack and Suzanne went to spend a few moments with Ryan. A helpful orderly directed Hunter and Marilyn to the waiting room just outside the huge surgery suite. Jack and Suzanne joined them a few minutes later. "It's going to be hours, unless— well, unless something happens," she said as she sat down beside Marilyn. "You two can go on if you like. We'll be all right."

Hunter and Marilyn shook their heads instantly. "No, we'll wait with you," Hunter said.

Marilyn wandered down to the lobby and brought back three papers and a couple of paperback books to help kill a little of the long wait. Jack and Hunter read the papers and Suzanne and Marilyn made a stab at reading the paperbacks, but all four of them would stiffen every time the wide doors going into the suite would open and four sets of eyes would swing to the door, hoping that Ryan's doctor was not standing there. As the hours crept by and Dr. Gold did not appear, Marilyn felt herself beginning to grow hopeful. Maybe, just maybe Ryan had a chance. Maybe the little fellow could make it.

Lunchtime came and went. Hunter went out for hamburgers and Marilyn coaxed Jack and Suzanne to finish most of theirs.

Then as the clock was approaching three, the doors to the surgery suite flew open and Ryan's doctor stood there, a beaming smile on his face. "Well, you folks got your miracle," he said softly as Jack and Suzanne rushed over to him, tears of joy in their eyes. Hunter and Marilyn followed them a little more slowly.

"So how is Ryan, Dr. Gold?" Suzanne asked.

"A hell of a lot better than I ever thought possible," the doctor replied. "Oops, sorry, sir," he said to Hunter. "He must have been a lot stronger than we thought, because he pulled through just fine. He will never be a football star or be able to do manual labor, but with a sedentary life he'll do just fine."

"Oh, that's wonderful," Suzanne breathed as two big tears ran down her cheeks. "Thank you so much, doctor," she said.

"Yes, thank you," Jack Bohannon said, crying openly and not bothering to hide it. Hunter put his arm around the big man's shoulders and hugged him tightly.

"I think you folks ought to thank God too," the doctor admitted. "It wasn't entirely my skill in there that saved your little boy."

"Of course," Jack said as the doctor disappeared into the surgical suite. The four of them sat back down and bowed their heads. "We gave him into your care, Lord, feeling that he belonged with You," Jack said. "Thank you for returning him to us, healed and whole."

"Yes, thank you, Lord," Suzanne whispered, her face a wreath of joy.

"Yes, Lord," Marilyn whispered, her heart torn in two. Yes, she was grateful that Ryan was spared; she was sincerely grateful. But a part of her was jealous at the same time. Why was this child and his parents spared and her own child taken? She forced herself not to entertain such thoughts, and after Hunter's moving prayer she reached out and hugged Suzanne tightly. "I'm so happy that Ryan's all right," she said softly.

"I think I'm the happiest mother in the whole world," Suzanne bubbled joyfully.

The four of them chatted until a nurse from the surgical suite called to the Bohannons that they could see Ryan, and Hunter and Marilyn promised to call everyone in New Braunfels and tell them the good news.

As they left the hospital, Marilyn's resentment over Ryan's recovery returned to haunt her. Despising herself for even feeling such a thing, she followed Hunter out to the truck and got in, responding to Hunter's happy chatter with only half her mind. Of course she was glad that Ryan was spared, and that Jack and Suzanne would never know the piercing grief that she had known for almost two years. She wouldn't wish that on anyone. But why couldn't she have had the same chance extended to her and her son?

She sat quietly, answering Hunter in monosyllables, until he pulled into their driveway, then she hopped out of the truck and went in, heading for the kitchen. It was after five and she had to be on duty by seven.

As Hunter made several telephone calls, letting various people know Ryan's good news, Marilyn broiled steaks and opened a couple of cans of vegetables. She set two plates at the table and made a small tossed salad, and was serving the meal as Hunter walked back into the room. He pulled her close and kissed her cheek, then sat down to Marilyn's tasty meal. "If I'm not careful, I'm going to get my fat roll back from all your good cooking," he said as he spooned up a serving of green peas.

"I don't think you have to worry," Marilyn said absently as she put their tea glasses on the table. She bowed her head for Hunter's short blessing, then sat quietly, pushing her food around on her plate while Hunter hungrily wolfed down his steak.

"You know, it's days like today that make the ministry worthwhile," he said as he ate the last of his steak. Marilyn picked up his plate then hers still half-filled with her dinner and carried them to the sink. "It was so wonderful to be with those parents in their joy," Hunter continued. "Their strength was rewarded, don't you think?"

"I guess so," Marilyn said shortly as she filled the sink with water and methodically began washing the dishes.

"You can't tell me that Ryan's recovery wasn't an answer to prayer, now can you?" Hunter continued.

"Yes, I'm sure it was," Marilyn said evenly.

Hunter looked at her a little strangely. "Marilyn, aren't you excited about Ryan? You're awfully quiet, you know."

"Of course I'm excited," Marilyn said as she scrubbed the broiler. "I wouldn't wish the death of a child on anyone. I've been there, remember?"

"Then why are you so quiet?" Hunter asked, looking at her shrewdly.

"I don't want to talk about it," she said as she let the water out of the sink. "You know, I'm going to have to let you take some of this kitchen detail," she said musingly as she looked at her red hands. "I've got to get ready for work," she added as she headed for the bedroom.

"Don't try to change the subject," Hunter said firmly as he followed her out to the hall. "You've been as quiet as a mouse ever since we left San Antonio. Would you care to talk about it?"

"Not particularly," Marilyn said as she took her Sam Brown from the closet and climbed the stairs.

"Why not?" Hunter demanded, following her into the bedroom.

"Because I'm ashamed of the way that I feel," Marilyn admitted as she unbuttoned her blouse and pulled it off.

"And how is that?" Hunter asked her quietly, sitting on the side of the bed.

"Oh, Hunter, I'm glad that child lived. But why couldn't mine have lived too?" She pulled off her skirt and tossed it on the bed, then kicked off her shoes and pulled off her panty hose.

"Well, Marilyn, I don't think you can help feeling a little resentment; that's perfectly normal," Hunter said quietly. "Of course you wonder why yours couldn't have lived. And once again, I don't have the answer for you. But if it's any consolation, Suzanne Bohannon can't have any more children. If she had lost Ryan, that would have been it for her. At least you can have more. You can have a child by me. In fact," he said softly, "I hope you do have a child by me, very soon."

Marilyn's hands froze in the act of taking her uniform shirt out of the wardrobe. "What do you mean, I can have another child?" she ground out coldly.

"Just that," Hunter said firmly. "Oh, Marilyn," he said as he took her arms and held them gently, "you can have another child of your own."

"And that's supposed to make up for losing Bobby?" Marilyn spat as she jerked loose from Hunter's grasp and whirled away from him. With trembling fingers she pulled on her blouse and fastened the snaps. "Damn it, Hunter, I don't want any more children!"

Hunter paled beneath his honeymoon tan. "You don't want any more?" he asked ominously.

"Of course not," Marilyn said angrily as she pulled on her uniform pants.

"So what have you been doing about it?" he asked. "We haven't used anything to prevent one."

"I went back on the pill," Marilyn said.

"Without even telling me?" Hunter demanded. "Why?"

"You know why," Marilyn said derisively. "I didn't want to get pregnant with another child. You act like I can have another baby and that will make losing Bobby all right. Well, it won't, Hunter. A child isn't like a puppy or a turtle that you can replace when one dies. Don't you understand? Bobby was a little person, with thoughts and ideas and—and... Oh, Hunter, of course I don't want any more children! They wouldn't be Bobby, don't you see?"

"My God, I don't believe you," Hunter bit out scathingly. "Yes, you suffered a crushing blow when your son was killed. But you have another chance. You could have a child, be a mother again. No, our child wouldn't be Bobby, but he or she would be a person in his or her own right!"

"I don't want that person in his or her own right!" Marilyn screamed at Hunter. "I don't want some other child! I want Bobby!"

"Well, you can't *have* Bobby!" Hunter yelled back furiously. "Marilyn, Bobby is *gone!* Do you hear me? *Gone!*" Marilyn recoiled from the harsh cruelty of Hunter's words. "And you're prepared to throw away another chance for happiness because it can't be exactly as you want it. You know, Marilyn, I don't think you really want that second chance at living." Hunter stuck his hands into his pockets and paced the room slowly, Marilyn's shocked eyes following him as he walked the room. "You don't want to have a full life again. You would rather stay right where I found you five months ago, buried alive in your grief. I was right about you. You are a coward."

Marilyn stared at Hunter, her face pale with pain from the cruel words he had spoken. Then she turned to the mirror and started pinning up her hair. "You're right, Hunter," she said slowly, the anger draining out of her to be replaced by defeat. "I am a coward. I don't want to live that kind of full life again because it just hurts too much if anything happens. I'm sorry, but I think I've taken just about all the pain I can stand, thank you." Marilyn retouched her makeup with trembling fingers, then sat down on the bed and started pulling on her socks, avoiding the eyes of the man she loved and that she knew she was hurting with each word she spoke. "Hunter, I don't want any more children because it hurts too much when you lose them."

"You wouldn't lose another one," Hunter argued quietly.

"How do I know that?" Marilyn demanded.

"Marilyn, what happened to Bobby was a freak accident! The statistical chances of something like that—"

"Can you give me a guarantee that nothing would ever happen to a child of mine again?" she asked matter-of-factly.

"Of course not," Hunter replied impatiently. "You know there are never any guarantees in this life."

"I rest my case," Marilyn replied quietly. She stepped into her boots and laced on her Sam Brown. "I'm sorry, Hunter. It just hurts too much to risk that kind of heartache again. Every time I would look at that child I'd wonder—are you going to die and hurt me too?"

"You risked marrying again," Hunter pointed out slowly. "Why not risk a child?"

Marilyn shrugged, unwilling to admit she had fallen in love with him against her will. "It's not the same," she said slowly. "That child is a part of you, your flesh. Losing a child is like losing a part of yourself. So if you think I'm risking that kind of hurt and loss by letting myself love another child, you've got a screw loose somewhere up there. Yes, Hunter, I prefer not to live again, if living means loving and losing. It hurts less that way." She picked up her hat and put it on, then picked up her jacket and headed for the front door. "I'll be in before dawn," she said quietly as she pulled the front door shut behind her and walked to the pickup truck.

Well, you certainly had your talk with Hunter, she told herself as she backed the truck out of the driveway and headed toward the office. Her hands were shaking and she had a splitting headache, but surprisingly her eyes were dry. Yes, she was sure that in Hunter's eyes she was a coward for not wanting another child, and she was sure that Hunter was hurt and disappointed that she wouldn't give him one. *But I just can't risk it,* she told herself. *I have risked enough by loving and marrying Hunter, knowing that I could lose him someday. I just can't risk loving and losing Hunter's child too.*

Hunter stared in shock at Marilyn's retreating back as she shut the door to the bedroom and walked firmly down the stairs. He peeked out the window and watched her drive away, then sat on the bed and buried his head in his hands. He had thought she was over her obsession with Bobby, that she was going to be all right, and the knowledge that she wasn't had dealt him a crushing blow. *I just can't believe that she still feels that way,* Hunter agonized as he hauled himself to his feet and wandered out of the bedroom. *Oh, Marilyn, I wanted you to give me a child,* he thought sadly as he wandered through the empty parsonage. *A little boy with my eyes, your hair. Or a little blond girl that would have pretty legs like yours when she grew up. I thought I could make you whole again so that you would want my child, and I couldn't. You don't want it. Oh, why haven't I been able to bring you out of your grief back into a full life?*

Taking a deep breath, Hunter entered his lonely study and sat down to his sermon notes for Sunday. Pride. Good topic, he thought as he sat down to read through his file.

He read at first quickly, gleaning material to put into the sermon, but as he went deeper and deeper into the file his reading rate slowed and his sermon was forgotten. Pride. Arrogance. Wasn't that exactly what he had been guilty of with Marilyn? He had seen her and desired her, and when he had found out that she had retreated into grief, he had set out single-handedly to force her back into the mainstream of life. He had hounded her to play for the church, had forced her into the sensual realm with his passionate embrace, had asked her to face yet more grief with the Bohannons, and then had the audacity to suggest that she have another child by him. And never once had he asked himself if she was ready for the next step, or if what he was doing was for himself or for her. He had never even whispered a prayer asking God to help Marilyn overcome her grief, or even asked the Almighty for guidance in dealing with her.

You were arrogant in the extreme, Hunter told himself as he stared at his sermon file unseeingly. *It wasn't your place to decide that Marilyn should be over her grief, or to try to bring her out of it yourself. Only God could provide that kind of healing, and He would have in His own time if you hadn't interfered. Oh, Marilyn, I've failed you,* he thought miserably as two large tears rolled down his cheeks. *I tried to do it myself, and that was wrong, and now you're even more hurt than ever. What on earth can I do to salvage this mess?*

Don't depend on your own wisdom, Hunter, he cautioned himself as he stared with haunted eyes at the swaying bushes outside the window. *That's how you got into this in the first place. You better call on someone who is wiser than you.* Thoroughly humbled, Hunter bowed his head and prayed fervently for Marilyn, and for guidance for himself in the days ahead.

CHAPTER TEN

Marilyn sat on the bench at Landa Park and watched the small train chug by, full of mothers and fathers taking their little ones on a Saturday afternoon excursion. The sound of laughter spilled out into the unseasonably warm afternoon, and Marilyn smiled faintly as the sunlight warmed her face and the breeze blew a few strands of the hair that had escaped from her chignon. Although she had been off duty for an hour or more, she had no desire to go back to the parsonage just yet. Hunter was spending the day in San Antonio on business, and the house was horribly lonely when his vibrant presence was not there to fill it.

Marilyn watched the train round the curve and disappear into the trees. Bobby used to love to ride that train, she remembered, waiting for the familiar stab of pain to appear that she felt whenever she remembered her son. It did, of course, but it was not the blinding, tearing sort of pain that she had felt for so many months. It was more of a fleeting pain, a what-might-have-been sort of pain, the pain of regret. But it was not the pain that had torn her apart for so long.

Am I getting over Bobby? Marilyn asked herself as she watched a young mother and her pudgy little daughter buying tickets for the next train ride. The little girl toddled along beside the young woman, holding her mother's hand tightly, red curls bouncing in the breeze, her sticky fingers busily exploring everything they could touch. Marilyn watched the child closely, testing herself. Would the anguish that she had felt for so long when she saw other people's children come today? The little girl fidgeted impatiently as her mother bought the tickets, then sat wiggling beside her mother until the next train appeared. The woman got on the train with the child, and Marilyn watched them until the train had disappeared around the bend.

It didn't hurt all that much, Marilyn thought with a shock. *I could watch that child without going to pieces.* But she did envy the mother. That mother had a child to take on the train today, and Marilyn didn't. *I wish I had a little child to bring here this afternoon,* she thought wistfully.

Picking up her hat, she walked slowly to the pickup truck and climbed inside, driving slowly back to the parsonage. She let herself in the empty house and shed her uniform, then pulled on a pair of jeans and a shirt. She made a glass of iced tea, then wandered out on the patio and stared at the huge backyard with its old pecan trees towering as tall as the two-story house. *This yard would be a great place for children to play,* she thought as she watched a sparrow busily building a nest. She scuffed her bare feet on the flagstones and sipped her tea, letting her thoughts return to the harsh argument she and Hunter had almost a week ago, and the quiet truce they had shared ever since.

Hunter's words had cut deeply, but Marilyn had to acknowledge that there was a lot of truth in them. Bobby was gone and he wasn't coming back, but she still had a chance to have a family. She had another husband, a wonderful one this time, and he desperately wanted her to give him a child. Hunter had been waiting up for her when she got off duty that morning and he had taken her into his arms and made love to her tenderly, but neither of them had dared broach the subject of the argument. Marilyn had gone back several times to see Ryan and Suzanne and had found that her generous spirit had overcome the resentment she felt on the day of Ryan's surgery. Too, her resentment was tempered by the thought that Ryan's life would be somewhat limited, a fact that she had ignored that day at the hospital. He would never be able to be fully active or do all the things that most children did. So the Bohannons didn't get off scot-free, she had to admit. There would still be problems in their life.

So what about her own life? Marilyn swallowed the last of the tea and set the glass down on the flagstones. Did she want to have another child even though it wouldn't be Bobby? Could she accept another child and love it the way she had her son? Her thoughts returned to the little girl and her mother at the park. She had envied that mother because she had a child to take to the park this afternoon, but she had not been thinking particularly about Bobby. She had just been lonely for a child. Any child. Marilyn gulped as her eyes filled with tears. Hunter's child.

The face of her husband swam before her and she pictured tall blond boys running and playing in this huge backyard. She let her imagination go further and she could see in her mind's eye a little girl this time, with dark curls like her own, toddling across the floor and reaching out for a toy. They would grow older, go to school, get bicycles for Christmas, graduate, go to college, get married, bring her grandchildren. And Hunter would be beside her, loving the children that they had together.

But what if something happened to one of them, as it had Bobby? Marilyn instantly recoiled from that. *It would kill me,* she thought. But that's the risk you have to take, she reminded herself. Every parent takes that risk. And, too, if the horror ever happened again, she would have Hunter beside her this time. She would have him grieving with her, pulling with her. She wouldn't have to go through it alone.

But was she ready yet to take on loving another child? Was she ready to put the past completely behind her and start over? To an extent she already had, by marrying Hunter. But was she ready to take that final step? She just did not know.

Her thoughts whirling, she was putting her tea glass in the sink when the front door opened and Hunter came in. Smiling gently, Marilyn opened her arms and Hunter stepped into them, hugging her tightly. She returned his embrace, feeling the strong warmth of the man she now loved with all her heart. *If I love him like this, surely I could love the child we would have together,* she thought as Hunter released her.

"So how have you spent the afternoon?" Hunter asked as he produced a small box from his pocket.

"What's this?" Marilyn asked as he handed her the box.

"I saw those downtown and thought you might like them," Hunter replied as she flipped open the box containing a pair of silver filigree earrings. "I thought they might look nice with your uniform," he teased.

"Oooh, I love them," Marilyn cooed. Of course, she could not wear them in uniform, but they would look perfect with most of her dresses and skirts. "You're spoiling me, Hunter." *He would be like this with his children,* she thought suddenly. If he could treat her this way, when he didn't even love her, what a father he would make to the children he did love!

"That's all right. You need spoiling," Hunter replied softly. "So, woman, what's for supper?"

"Chicken again," she admitted. "It was on sale this week."

Hunter kissed her again and wandered toward the study, Marilyn's eyes following his retreating back. He had said nothing about the argument, but this past week she had caught glimpses of real pain in his eyes when he thought she was not looking. *I hurt him horribly last week and he can still bring me a present,* she thought as she reached up and put on the earrings.

And do I have any right to refuse him children, she asked herself later that night as she lay awake, watching with gentle eyes the sleeping man beside her. He had made tender passionate love to her, as he always did, but although her body was relaxed and satisfied, her mind was in a spin. She had taken the plunge and married again, and this marriage was happy, secure, better than before. Was it possible that the same would be true of another child?

Not better, she told herself, but certainly as happy. She would love Hunter's child. If her first marriage had been better, she would have had more children and loved them. She owed it to herself and her husband to have a family. *And you owe it to Hunter to tell him the truth about how you feel about him,* she thought as she watched Hunter's chest rise and fall. *You love him and he has a right to know that. Maybe, if he knows you love him, he'll learn to love you someday.*

Should I wake him up and tell him? she wondered. *Or tell him in the morning?* But as she tried to think of a way to come out and tell Hunter all that was in her heart, she realized that she had one more thing that she had to do before she could start her new life. Promising herself that she would talk to Hunter just as soon as she had done this one last task, she turned over and went to sleep.

The next afternoon, after Marilyn got off duty, she went by the florist shop that was close to the office and bought a small spray of daisies. She drove to the cemetery and parked her truck, then picked up the flowers and walked slowly into the cemetery, clutching the vase tightly in her hand. She stopped in front of Bobby's headstone and looked down at the simple marker that she had put up for her child. She stared at the headstone for long moments, tears clouding her eyes as she told her son good-bye.

I have to let you go, son. You don't belong with me anymore. You're where you belong, and so am I, so although I will always love you, I'm letting you go in my heart.

I've married again, Bobby. I wasn't happy with your dad, and sooner or later you would have been able to tell that, and it would have hurt you. But I'm happy now, Bobby. I love Hunter. He wants me to have a family with him, and I'm going to do that. It doesn't mean that I love you any less—it's because I loved you so much that I want that kind of happiness once again. I need to love my new husband and have children by him. But I'll never forget you, son. Never.

Marilyn knelt and brushed the stray leaves that had blown against the marker and placed the vase of flowers in front of the small stone. "Good-bye, Bobby," she whispered softly as she brushed a tear from her eye. Then she got up and slowly walked back toward the truck, her heart at real peace for the first time in almost two years.

Hunter locked the door of the church behind him and hurried toward the car, since Marilyn was off duty by now and was probably already at home. Hunter frowned to himself when he thought of the awful argument they had had the day of Ryan's surgery. Although Marilyn had not acted angry about it later, she had said nothing about the bitter truths they had hurled at each other and had given him no clue as to how she really felt about what had been said.

Hunter rubbed the space between his eyes and walked to the car, then froze as he saw the big yellow pickup truck pull up at the cemetery and Marilyn get out carrying a vase of flowers. *Oh, no, she's going there to grieve for Bobby,* Hunter thought grimly as he watched her walk through the cemetery and stand for long moments staring down at the gravestone of her son. *She's back to square one,* Hunter thought miserably, *and my interference put her there. She's just as buried in her grief as she was the day she played for that wedding last fall.*

Hunter's heart contracted in pain as he watched her reach down and brush the leaves away from the stone and place the flowers in front of it. *It's hopeless,* he thought. *She's never going to get over that child. She's never going to be able to give me one of our own.* His eyes filling with tears, Hunter got into the Mustang and roared out of the parking lot, finding the nearest highway that led out of town. He didn't know where it led and he really didn't care, just as long as it didn't lead back to Marilyn. He didn't think he was ready to face her just yet, now that he knew the state of her heart.

"Hunter?" Marilyn called as she threw open the door to the parsonage and walked inside. "Are you here?" she asked as she wandered in and shut the door behind her. Hunter's car wasn't in the driveway, but that didn't mean anything, since he frequently left it at the church. She wandered through the house, and realizing that Hunter wasn't at home, took a shower and put on a pretty jumpsuit and her new earrings.

Glancing at the clock, she decided that she better go ahead and start supper, since it was late and Hunter would be home soon. He had only planned to do paperwork in the church office this afternoon, and he never stayed there past five. It was already six, and he was bound to be getting hungry. Marilyn busied herself in the kitchen and fixed a simple quiche, but she still had not heard from Hunter, and it was nearly seven. Irritation combined with the first stirrings of anxiety. If he had been held up, why hadn't he let her know?

Putting the quiche and the salad in the refrigerator, Marilyn busied herself with chores around the house until almost eight, reassuring herself that Hunter would walk through the door at any minute. Finally exasperation combined with real worry prompted her to get into the truck and drive the three blocks to the church. She parked her truck and got out, disappointed not to find the Mustang and even more disappointed to find the church doors locked. She peered in the windows of Hunter's office just to make sure, but there was no sign of him.

Where is he? Marilyn asked herself, her worry getting the better of her anger. *Why hasn't he let me know where he is?* With trembling hands she drove the truck back to the parsonage and went inside, calling Hunter's name in case he had come home while she was away. The sound of her voice reverberated through the big old house, but Hunter did not answer.

Marilyn wandered into the study and flipped on the light. Maybe he had had an appointment that she had forgotten about. She checked his calendar and found no appointment listed, but she did find a notation to call the Bohannons and see how Ryan was doing.

Relief coursed through her as she picked up the telephone. Ryan was making such phenomenal progress that he might have come home today and Hunter might have been called on to provide transportation. The phone rang twice before Suzanne answered.

"Suzanne, this is Marilyn Templeton. May I speak to Hunter, please?"

"I'm sorry, Marilyn, Hunter's not here." Suzanne's voice sounded puzzled.

"He's not?" Marilyn asked weakly. "Have you heard from him?"

"Yes, early this morning when he called to check on Ryan. He offered to bring us home tomorrow, but Jack took the week off."

"Ryan's coming home tomorrow?" Marilyn asked.

"Yes, I'm here getting some clothes gathered up for him."

"That's great," Marilyn said sincerely. "Suzanne, are you sure you haven't seen Hunter?"

"No, Marilyn, I haven't," Suzanne assured her. "Is anything wrong?"

"Uh—I don't think so," Marilyn replied. "He just hasn't come home yet."

"Well, you know how it is," Suzanne said. "Men get to talking and forget the time sometimes. I wouldn't worry."

Sure, Marilyn thought as she hung up the telephone. Hunter wouldn't get to talking for four hours. It was nine o'clock. Something had to be wrong. Hunter was not the kind of man to not let her know that he was going to be that late. Frantically, she thought of calling the police and seeing if any accidents had been reported, then realized that everyone on the force knew Hunter and that she would have been the first one notified if he had been hurt. The same was true of the local hospitals. So he had not been in an accident.

But maybe he had driven into San Antonio and been hurt up there. His driver's license still read Houston, and they wouldn't know to contact her. Or what if he had driven over one of the guardrails and into Canyon Lake? *Oh, Hunter, if something happened to you, I don't think I could stand it!* she screamed inside, as she paced for the next two hours, growing more terrified by the minute.

Finally, almost beside herself with worry, Marilyn did the only thing she knew to do. She knelt in front of the shabby old sofa in the parlor and bent her head. At first she prayed silently, then her lips quietly formed the words that were in her heart. "Please let Hunter be all right. Oh, please let him be all right! Please give me another chance with Hunter, Lord, for I love him so much."

* * *

Hunter pulled into the driveway and killed the engine of his car. He had driven through the hill country for hours, stopping twice in small towns for gas, then had driven through Marble Falls and around the lake chain west of there and had stopped at a lookout point and watched the brilliant sunset. He had stared for long moments into the waters of the lake, trying to come to grips with the fact that his wife was still a prisoner of her grief. *I'll just have to love her,* Hunter thought as he watched the flaming ball dip slowly below the horizon. *That's all I can do, and if she ever recovers enough to love me in return, that will have to be enough for me.* He had driven a little more, stalling a little before he had to go back to Marilyn and take up his role as a loving husband, knowing that she could not love him in return.

Hunter climbed out of the car and walked slowly to the front door, wondering why the lights were still on in the parlor. Marilyn usually went to bed early when she was working the day shift, and it was well after eleven. He withdrew his key and unlocked the door as quietly as he could, in case Marilyn was asleep, and tiptoed into the entry hall. Peeking into the living room, he froze in anguish at the sight of his wife kneeling by the couch, her voice a quiet whisper of pain. Hunter crept closer, straining to hear Marilyn's heartbreaking prayer. He felt a little guilty about eavesdropping, but if he could find out what was in her thoughts, he might be able to help her.

At first her words were an indistinct mumble, but as he moved a little closer Hunter could hear something about loving someone very much, and about giving her a second chance. Hunter frowned in puzzlement. She couldn't be talking about Bobby. She knew that Bobby was gone. But she wanted a second chance? Had she changed her mind about not having children? Hunter moved a step closer and knelt down a little, then he strangled a cry in his throat when he finally heard what she was saying. She was praying for him! She was praying for his safe return! She was saying that she loved him!

Marilyn felt a gentle hand on her shoulder and froze in terror, then whipped around to see her husband leaning over her. Shock froze her for a moment, then she whispered his name in a choked voice. She reached up and touched him gently to make sure it was really him, then when he knelt down beside her she gathered him into her arms. "Hunter, are you all right? I've been so worried about you! Where have you been? Oh, Hunter!" she sobbed.

"Marilyn, I'm sorry," Hunter crooned lovingly. "I never meant to hurt you or to scare you," he said as he rocked her back and forth.

Slowly her sobbing stopped and she raised tear-stained eyes to his. "Where were you?" she asked miserably.

Hunter looked ashamed. "I needed to get away for a few hours. I honestly didn't think you'd worry, Marilyn."

"Of course I'd worry!" she exclaimed indignantly, drawing away from his embrace. "Why wouldn't I worry?"

"I didn't think you cared," Hunter admitted frankly.

"But I do," Marilyn replied softly, "because I love you."

"Yes, I heard you just now," Hunter said. "Did you mean it? Do you really?"

Marilyn nodded. "I sure didn't want to, but I fell in love with you in spite of myself." She stood up and faced Hunter squarely. "I wanted to love you about as much as I wanted to have more children," she admitted. "But I just couldn't help it. That's why I married you, Hunter. Because I love you."

"If you'll forgive me for saying so, it was worth blowing two tanks of gas to hear you say that," Hunter said as he stood beside her, looking deeply into her eyes. "But why on earth didn't you ever let me know?" he asked with genuine puzzlement.

"How could I? You started seeing me with the idea of fulfilling your obligations toward a grieving member of your congregation, and then you married me because you were lonely. Or maybe you thought you could help me by marrying me, I don't know. What was I supposed to say, 'Oh, by the way, Hunter, I seem to have fallen in love with you'?" Marilyn stared into his eyes, the genuine anguish on her face turning to astonishment when Hunter started laughing out loud.

"Marilyn, I'm sorry for laughing at you, but that is the funniest thing I've heard in a long time. My ministerial obligations? Lonely? Do I honestly strike you as the kind of man who would go so far as to marry someone just to fulfill my ministerial responsibilities? Do you honestly think I would marry a woman because I was lonely? I do have a television, you know."

"You mean you weren't just being nice?" Marilyn asked.

"What do you think I am, a saint? Would a man who is just being nice start daydreaming about his organist in the middle of a sermon, clean out his savings to buy his bride a diamond necklace, make love to her for most of the night? Or spend an hour and a half looking for the perfect pair of earrings? Or tremble every time you touch him?" Hunter reached out and touched Marilyn tenderly. "Nice had nothing to do with it. I love you, Marilyn. I've loved you ever since you fed me an omelette and understood my frustrations."

"Then why didn't you tell me?" Marilyn asked as she reached out to Hunter. "Why all that nonsense about being lonely, and having a good life together?"

"I didn't think you were ready to hear that I loved

you," Hunter said as he took her in his arms and held her tenderly. "You were still horribly grieved by your child's death and hurt by your failed marriage. I was afraid that if I told you I loved you, with all that that implies, you would run like a scared rabbit." He pulled her down on the couch. "That's why I did everything under the sun to get you back into the real world again. I was wrong to do that. I was selfish—I thought that if you were over your sorrow, that you might find a place in your life for me. It wasn't my place to try to heal your grief, and I'm sorry that my meddling has brought you more pain."

"It's brought pain, but it's brought healing, too, Hunter," Marilyn admitted quietly. "And there will always be a place in my life for the man I love."

She opened her arms to him and he moved into them, tears running down his cheeks as he held her to him tightly. *She loves me! She actually loves me in spite of the pain I brought her.* Raising his head, Hunter found her mouth and began kissing it gently, affirming with the tender touch of her lips on his that she really did love him. Good grief, why hadn't he recognized it sooner? It had been there every time she touched him.

Marilyn smiled into Hunter's eyes as he slowly pulled away from her. "Would you like to make love to the woman who loves you?" she asked softly.

"Would you like to make love to the man who loves you?" he asked softly.

Marilyn nodded as Hunter scooped her into his arms, linking them around her securely as he carried her up the stairs. Marilyn threw her arms around his neck and nibbled his cheek lightly as he carried her into their bedroom and laid her on the big bed. He leaned over and kissed her lingeringly as he pulled off his tie. "Will you do me the honors?" he asked as he extended his wrists to her.

Obligingly Marilyn unhooked the small cuff links and

put them on the nightstand, then she reached out and unbuttoned Hunter's shirt slowly as his lips nibbled hers, tempting her with their sweetness. She pushed his shirt off his shoulders and reached for the belt of his slacks, and with the expertise gained in the last month or so she swiftly took care of the belt buckle and the zipper, caressing him daringly as her fingers lowered the zipper, her knowing touch eliciting a gasp of surprised pleasure from Hunter. "You're going to have to take those off yourself," she whispered as she withdrew her tormenting fingers from his sensitive midsection.

Hunter pulled away from her and swiftly kicked off the slacks, then he sat down and peeled off his socks and shoes. "This was easier in Cancún," he complained as he unceremoniously pulled off his underwear, exposing his unclad body to Marilyn's eager gaze, her eyes feasting on the sensuous planes and lines that she found there. "We wore less down there."

"I knew there was a reason I missed that place," Marilyn murmured dryly.

Hunter reached over to Marilyn and slowly pulled down the zipper to her jumpsuit, his mouth faithfully following the gap made by the parting zipper. He completely unzipped the suit, then started to slowly peel it off, covering each freshly exposed inch of tender flesh with sensuous kisses that curled Marilyn's insides with delight, until he had taken the suit down to her toes. He pitched it across the room and felt for the hook of her bra, snapping it open with a newfound expertise and exposing her breasts to tantalize him with their tenderness. "Getting pretty good at that, aren't you?" she teased as Hunter ran a light questing finger between her breasts.

"This lady deputy that I know has been letting me practice on her," Hunter said as his gentle lips captured the sensitive tip of her nipple.

Marilyn cradled his head as he nibbled first one rosy peak and then the other, tempting them both into alluring hardness. She ran her fingers through his soft hair and whimpered a little under Hunter's hands as his lips became even more arousing, raising her to a sensitivity to his touch that amazed her. His hands were filled with gentleness and love, and Marilyn wondered how she could have been so blind as to not realize that Hunter loved her, and had loved her for a long time. Although he had not expressed himself with words, he had poured his love for her into every touch, every kiss, every caress they had shared. He would have had to love her to make love to her as he had in Cancún, to hold her as he was holding her now.

"Do you suppose it will be any different now?" Marilyn asked as Hunter stroked her stomach lovingly.

"You mean now that we know we love each other?" Hunter asked. "I don't know," he said as he caressed the soft inner skin of her thigh. "Probably not, since we loved each other then, but just didn't know it."

But Hunter was wrong, Marilyn thought later as she was reeling with pleasure at his loving touch. There was no real comparison in the way that she had felt before and the way she felt now. Before, she had loved Hunter and accepted his passion. But now, twisting freely in his arms as his lips and his fingers tormented her, she was conscious of the love that Hunter gave to her in his every touch, his every caress, and she knew that her love for him was conveyed to him at the same time.

Now when Hunter sought out the secret recesses of her warmth and stroked it lovingly, she knew that it was not just passion for her. She knew now that he was touching her with all the love in his heart, and she responded to that love with loving abandon of her own. *No, Hunter,* she thought as their lovemaking drew to the inevitable release, *what we had before is nothing compared to what we're feeling tonight. This is new to us,* she thought as he gently parted her legs and prepared her for the act of love. *We've never been here before, you and I.*

Finally, as Marilyn thought she could give no more love and take no more pleasure, Hunter moved over her and made her one with him, joining with her soul as well as her body. She moved in rhythm with him, carried to a plane on which she had never been before, seeing love as it was meant to be, a harmony of body and spirit and soul. As she and Hunter swirled together toward the heights, she tasted the joy, the feeling of oneness with Hunter that would be theirs for the rest of their lives. Tonight was only the beginning of their love. This moment would be repeated through the years, until neither of them would be able to remember a time without it. When she reached the sublime moment of pleasure she did not cry out, but gasped as her entire body trembled with the force of her love. Hunter did cry out, her name escaping his lips.

They lay still for long moments, savoring the intimacy of their embrace, then Hunter withdrew from her and began the ritual again, reaching out to his wife with loving tenderness, and feeling her respond to his sensitive touch with love and tenderness of her own. They moved more slowly and with less urgency this time, touching and teasing and kissing and stroking until his sensual caresses had rekindled the fire in Marilyn, then he was one with her again, the fires burning just as brightly as they had before.

Long hours later Marilyn raised sleepy eyes to Hunter. "I love you," she whispered as she kissed his lips softly.

"I love you too," Hunter replied as he pushed her into the pillows and kissed her lingeringly. Although the physical side of her nature was sated, Marilyn's spirit was enflamed by the love in Hunter's kiss, and she responded to his caresses lovingly. "And I was wrong about it being the same, wasn't I?" he said musingly.

"Just think—we have this to look forward to for the rest of our lives," Marilyn mused as her stomach gave way with an embarrassing rumble.

Hunter laughed. "Sounds like you haven't eaten for hours," he teased.

"I haven't," Marilyn said in surprise. "I waited supper for you."

"And I wasn't here to eat it with you," Hunter chided himself. He looked at her beseechingly. "I haven't eaten for hours either," he hinted broadly.

Marilyn laughed. "For a man who can't cook worth a darn, you sure know how to eat!" she teased. "Oh, well, from the sublime to the ridiculous," she said as she got out of bed, clad only in her new earrings, a delightful sight as she unselfconsciously turned on a small lamp and hunted around for her robe. She tossed Hunter his and belted hers around her middle, then skipped down the stairs two at time and went to see what she could salvage of their supper.

Hunter followed her ten minutes later, his hair damp and glistening from the shower. Surprisingly, the quiche had not dried out and had warmed up nicely, and Marilyn had found some dressing for the salad. She poured them each a glass of milk and they made quick work of their four-in-the-morning feast, their love for each other shining in their eyes.

As Marilyn piled the last of the dishes in the sink, she turned to Hunter with a puzzled frown on her face. "I know that all's well that ends well, but why did you leave this afternoon in the first place? You've never wanted to get away from me before."

Hunter reached out and pulled Marilyn into his lap, burying his face in her hair. "I saw you at the cemetery with flowers for Bobby. I had thought you were getting over your horrible grief for your son. I honestly thought you were going to be able to put it behind you, and when I saw you there I realized that you hadn't, and it tore me apart." He ran his hands up and down her arms. "I'm selfish, I guess. I thought that maybe if you were grieving Bobby less, you might come to love me someday."

"But I do love you, Hunter," Marilyn admonished him gently. "After tonight you ought to know that."

"Then why were you at the cemetery this afternoon?" Hunter asked quietly.

Marilyn swallowed a lump in her throat. "I went and told Bobby good-bye," she said softly. "I was finally able to let him go." She turned around and stared into Hunter's eyes, her own smiling. "He's where he belongs now, and so am I. I've let him go, and I want to go forward now, with you."

"How far forward?" Hunter asked, holding his breath.

"All the way, Hunter. If you still want to, I want to have your child."

"Children," Hunter corrected her gently. "At least two."

Marilyn smiled softly. "I'd like that," she said sincerely.

"Oh, Marilyn, are you sure?" Hunter asked, holding her face between his hands and looking deeply into her eyes. "Honestly, I don't expect it. You were so vehement the other night."

"I didn't realize that I have been healed of my grief when we argued the other night," Marilyn replied. "I didn't realize it, but the pain is fading. Oh, it's not gone and it may never be entirely. And I'll never completely forget Bobby. But I want a family again. Not just a husband, wonderful though you are. A family."

"How do you feel about Bobby now?" Hunter asked tenderly. "I want you to be very sure about this."

"I'm at peace about him, Hunter."

"Then I'd say you're ready," Hunter said as Marilyn hopped off his lap and took him by the hand.

"Come on then. You get to help me with this." She led him up the stairs and into the bathroom, and handed him one packet of pills as she took the other remaining one. "Dr. Cooke would only give me three months worth," she said as she started popping the pills into the basin.

"He probably figured you'd change your mind," Hunter replied as he popped the pills out of the other packet.

Marilyn turned on the water and together they watched the pills dissolve and disappear down the drain. Then, their arms around each other, Hunter and Marilyn walked toward the big bed and crawled in, holding each other tightly.

Hunter drifted off to sleep immediately, but Marilyn lay in the still darkness, watching as the dark of night gave way to the promise of morning, her heart grateful for the joyous future that she had found in this loving man and the God whom he worshipped. As the night gave way to dawn, she shut her eyes and went to sleep, warmed by the tender healing that Hunter's love had brought to her life.

LOOK FOR NEXT MONTH'S
CANDLELIGHT ECSTASY ROMANCES ®

226 SPECIAL DELIVERY, *Elaine Raco Chase*
227 BUSINESS BEFORE PLEASURE, *Alison Tyler*
228 LOVING BRAND, *Emma Bennett*
229 THE PERFECT TOUCH, *Tate McKenna*
230 HEAVEN'S EMBRACE, *Sheila Paulos*
231 KISS AND TELL, *Paula Hamilton*
232 WHEN OPPOSITES ATTRACT, *Candice Adams*
233 TROUBLE IN PARADISE, *Antoinette Hale*

Candlelight Ecstasy Romances

210	**LOVERS' KNOT**, Hayton Monteith	15080-9-77
211	**TENDER JOURNEY**, Margaret Dobson	18556-4-19
212	**ALL OUR TOMORROWS**, Lori Herter	10124-7-19
213	**LOVER IN DISGUISE**, Gwen Fairfax	15086-8-14
214	**TENDER DECEPTION**, Heather Graham	18591-2-16
215	**MIDNIGHT MAGIC**, Barbara Andrews	15618-1-37
216	**WINDS OF HEAVEN**, Karen Whittenburg	19578-0-29
217	**ALL OR NOTHING**, Lori Copeland	10120-4-13
218	**STORMY SURRENDER**, Jessica Massey	18340-5-10
219	**MOMENT TO MOMENT**, Bonnie Drake	15791-9-10
220	**A CLASSIC LOVE**, Jo Calloway	11242-7-22
221	**A NIGHT IN THE FOREST**, Alysse Rasmussen	16399-4-22
222	**SEDUCTIVE ILLUSION**, Joanne Bremer	17722-7-28
223	**MORNING'S PROMISE**, Emily Elliott	15829-X-32
224	**PASSIONATE PURSUIT**, Eleanor Woods	16843-0-16
225	**ONLY FOR LOVE**, Tira Lacy	16676-4-18

$1.95 each

At your local bookstore or use this handy coupon for ordering.

DELL BOOKS　　　　　　　　　　　　　　　　　　　　B155A
P.O. BOX 1000, PINE BROOK, N.J. 07058-1000

Please send me the books I have checked above. I am enclosing $_____ (please add 75c per copy to cover postage and handling). Send check or money order—no cash or C.O.D.s. Please allow up to 8 weeks for shipment.

Name _____

Address _____

City _____ State Zip _____

- ☐ 13 **BODY AND SOUL**, Anna Hudson 10759-8-11
- ☐ 14 **CROSSFIRE**, Eileen Bryan 11599-X-39
- ☐ 15 **WHERE THERE'S SMOKE...**, Nell Kincaid 19417-2-16
- ☐ 16 **PAYMENT IN FULL**, Jackie Black 16828-7-15
- ☐ 17 **RED MIDNIGHT**, Heather Graham 17431-7-12
- ☐ 18 **A HEART DIVIDED**, Ginger Chambers 13509-5-18
- ☐ 19 **SHADOW GAMES**, Elise Randolph 17764-2-19
- ☐ 20 **JUST HIS TOUCH**, Emily Elliott 14411-6-39

$2.50 each

 At your local bookstore or use this handy coupon for ordering:

B155B

DELL BOOKS
P.O. BOX 1000, PINE BROOK, N.J. 07058-1000

Please send me the books I have checked above. I am enclosing $_____ (please add 75c per copy to cover postage and handling). Send check or money order—no cash or C.O.D.'s. Please allow up to 8 weeks for shipment.

Name _____

Address _____

City _____ State/Zip _____

If you enjoy squirming
through scary books,
you'll shiver through the stories of

MARY HIGGINS CLARK

☐ THE CRADLE WILL FALL	11545-0-18	$3.95
☐ A CRY IN THE NIGHT	11065-3-26	3.95
☐ A STRANGER IS WATCHING	18127-5-43	3.95
☐ WHERE ARE THE CHILDREN	19593-4-38	3.50

DELL BOOKS B155C
P.O. BOX 1000, PINE BROOK, N.J. 07058-1000

Please send me the books I have checked above. I am enclosing $_____ (please add 75¢ per copy to cover postage and handling). Send check or money order—no cash or C.O.D.'s. Please allow up to 8 weeks for shipment.

Mr. Mrs. Miss _____

Address _____

City _____ State/Zip _____

MARIANNE HARVEY

Know the passions and perils, the love and the lust, as the best of the past is reborn in her books.

☐ STORMSWEPT	19030-4-13	$3.50
☐ THE DARK HORSEMAN	11758-5-44	3.50
☐ THE PROUD HUNTER	17098-2-32	3.50
☐ THE WILD ONE	19207-2-02	2.95

Writing as Mary Williams

☐ GYPSY FIRES	12860-9-13	2.95
☐ GYPSY LEGACY	12990-7-16	2.95

DELL BOOKS
P.O. BOX 1000, PINE BROOK, N.J. 07058-1000

B155D

Please send me the books I have checked above. I am enclosing $_____$ (please add 75c per copy to cover postage and handling). Send check or money order—no cash or C.O.D.'s. Please allow up to 8 weeks for shipment.

Mr. Mrs. Miss _____

Address _____

City _____ State/Zip _____

The book that is revolutionizing
child care in America!

FEED YOUR KIDS RIGHT

Lendon Smith, M.D.

Here is Dr. Smith's complete, easy-to-follow program that clearly explains how you can help your child achieve his optimum physical and psychological health.

Discover how to:
- cure allergies, rashes, bedwetting
- prevent hyperactivity and stress
- stop colds and lessen the impact of childhood diseases
- rate the state of your child's health

This indispensable guide contains all the information you need to keep your family healthy and happy from infancy through adolescence.

A Dell Book $3.95   (12706-8)

At your local bookstore or use this handy coupon for ordering:

| DELL BOOKS   FEED YOUR KIDS RIGHT $3.95   (12706-8)
P.O. BOX 1000, PINE BROOK, N.J. 07058-1000   B155E

Please send me the above title. I am enclosing $ _____ (please add 75c per copy to cover postage and handling). Send check or money order—no cash or C.O.D.'s. Please allow up to 8 weeks for shipment.

Mr. Mrs. Miss _____

Address _____

City _____ State Zip _____